PIER
HEAD
JUMP

By the same author
COOL HAND LUKE

PIER HEAD JUMP

By Donn Pearce

The Bobbs-Merrill Company, Inc.
Indianapolis and New York

The Bobbs-Merrill Company, Inc.
Publishers   Indianapolis/New York
Copyright © 1972 by Donn Pearce
All rights reserved
Library of Congress catalog card number 77–173206
Printed in the United States of America

Designed by
TERRY REID

PIER
HEAD
JUMP

● THE LAST JOB CALL had been made at four. But a few men stayed behind to shoot pool, to talk, to watch TV or to get a haircut, some hoping for some late emergency job to come in before they closed the hall entirely at six. Cooper sprawled in an upholstered reading chair, his legs straight out, his hands clasped over his stomach, his head slumped with his chin snuggled against his shoulder. A group of Puerto Ricans were happily arguing over their pinochle game. There was the slow, clumsy tapping of a typewriter as the dispatcher registered a new man on the shipping list. A telephone rang. In a few minutes the typewriter resumed its tapping. The emergency exit door opened and closed with a rattle and a bang. Cooper's eyes opened and then squinched with pain. A tall, sweating fat man wearing an aloha shirt dropped a dirty seabag and a battered suitcase at his feet. He breathed rapidly, swallowed and let out a long sigh. Picking up his gear, he staggered over to the counter, talking to the dispatcher in a voice that carried all over the room.

Hey, McFinlay! I gotta ship out. I mean right *now*.

The dispatcher looked up from his typewriter and shifted the toothpick in his mouth.

Whiskey Bill! I just shipped you out a few days ago.

Look, McFinlay. Will you cut out the god-damn conversation and *do* somethin'? I need *another* job. *Now*.

The dispatcher put the toothpick deep into a crevice of the gum surrounding his lower right canine tooth, holding it at an upright angle, his little finger curled.

Huh. You're a lucky bastard, Whiskey. As a matter of

fact, I was just gonna go around the hall. Ten seconds ago I got this call for two replacements. Some jerk Bedroom Steward spilled a pitcher of boiling water from the coffee urn all over his neck and arm. They had to take him off. But then. This stupid A.B. gets so excited helpin' him down the gangway with his stuff and all. Damned if he don't trip and break his leg. So then *both* of 'em ends up in the Marine Hospital.

Never mind the details. Write me out a shippin' ticket.

The dispatcher sucked at his teeth as the fat man fumbled under the tail of his aloha shirt for his wallet.

It's a Liberty ship. The *Ocean Endeavor*. Goin' to the Far East with military cargo. Manila first. And maybe Saigon.

Listen. I just don't give a shit.

Cooper raised his head. He sat up straight, thought a moment and then went over to the counter, his hand nervous as he ran his fingers through his hair.

Hey. Did I hear you guys talkin' about a job?

Yeah. I'm lookin' for an A.B. It's a pier head jump.

Yeah. Okay. I'll take it.

How long will it take you to get your gear together?

I got it downstairs in the baggage room.

The dispatcher checked Cooper's papers and took his ten-day-old registration card. He glanced at the back of the Merchant Mariner's Document issued by the Coast Guard to make sure he had an endorsement as an able bodied seaman.

You got one of them officer's endorsements. Any-unlicensed-rating-in-the-deck-department. You got a mate's license or what?

Yeah. I got one. But I never sail under it.

Year? Well. Anyway. Here's what you guys do. Jump in a taxi and go over and see Doctor Haiffen. 42 Beaver Street. Then take your fit-for-duty slips over to the Shipping Commissioner. After he signs you on the Articles, go right down to the ship. Fast. She's tied up at Pier 3. Brooklyn Army Base. The pilot and the tugs are standin' by now.

Hey, McFinlay, complained the fat man. I thought for Christ's sake this was an emergency. We got to go all the hell over to *Manhattan?* Just to see a stupid doctor? And *then* to the Army Base? That's in the opposite fuckin' direction.

The dispatcher led them downstairs and across the parking lot to a converted private garage that the union used as a baggage room. He took Cooper's numbered check and hunted through the piles and stacks until he located a recently scrubbed seabag, the eyelets reinforced with handmade stitches of sail twine, the braided lanyard decorated with fancy Turk's heads and elaborate splices. The dispatcher slowly searched over the platform shelves, glancing several times at the number on the deck stub.

It's a cardboard box. I got my radio in it.

Shifting his toothpick, the dispatcher climbed a short ladder and handed down a dirty, chaffed cardboard carton wrapped with several turns of manila rope. Gingerly Cooper reached up to take it down.

It's a Phillips. International shortwave. Cost me damn near three hundred bucks.

Whiskey Bill called out from another corner.

Hey, McFinlay. Right here. If that slow-ass Liberty is goin' halfway 'round the world, I'd better bring my trunk.

The medium-size steamer trunk had wheels fitted on one end like those sample cases pushed through the traffic of New York's commercial districts. Whiskey Bill trundled it across the parking lot as Cooper waved down a taxi. The driver opened the luggage compartment. Helping Bill with the enormous weight, Cooper lifted one end, grunting and gasping as they slid it inside.

Man. Christ. What the hell you got in this thing?

3

Whaddaya mean? Just my gear is all.

They got in the back seat, Cooper cradling the cardboard box in his lap. The rear end of the taxi sagged low and leaned to one side as the driver pulled away. With embarrassment Cooper asked Whiskey Bill if he could owe him his half of the fare.

Forget it. Man. I'm so glad to just get away from this town I'd pay *any*thing. What I ought to do is ask that crooked son-of-a-bitch doctor, Haiffen, to examine my head. And see if he can find out why I been wastin' my whole life associatin' with all these nutty seagoin' characters. Like that McFinlay? You think maybe *he* ain't nuts? Sittin' there like God pickin' his teeth? Listen. I've *sailed* with that guy. Years ago. Long before he happened to get in good with Bull Williams and got to be a Pie Card. Now he tries to act like some kind of a labor official. Hell. I knew McFinlay when he was a plain-ass oiler on this Knot ship we were on. One of them missile ship jobs. Christ. We're out there driftin' around in the South Atlantic for a month at a time in one *spot*. Finally we tie up at St. Helena Island. At our base, see? Only the Limeys wouldn't let nobody go ashore.

The taxi turned the corner at Prospect Avenue, heading for the Gowanus Parkway. Cooper's eyelids were half closed, staring at the dingy storefronts, the vacant lots littered with trash, the pedestrians, the parked cars. Again he had a ship. A place to eat and sleep. A place to earn some money.

The cab driver maneuvered through the traffic, stopping for red lights, pulling around cars slowing to make a turn. But he kept glancing up into the rearview mirror as Whiskey Bill went on with his story, his legs crossed, one hand gesticulating with short waves, pointing fingers, a loosely clenched fist.

So there was nothin' for us to do. See? So what we did do was, we all got drunk. We got some booze off this bumboat that comes paddlin' alongside and we had ourselves a private party. Well. I don't remember how it all started, exactly. But the next thing I know, all of us are out there on deck and we're havin' a tattoo contest. Guys are rollin' up their sleeves and showin' these names of girl friends and U.S. Navy Forever and Death Before Dishonor and all that crap. But next thing you know the shirts start comin' off. And here's sailin' ships and hula dancers and pirates and clowns and Indian chiefs and I don't know what all.

Whiskey Bill began to laugh, his enormous belly jiggling beneath the folds of the red, yellow, orange, lavender and green floral pattern of the aloha shirt.

But then one guy lets out this real defiant screech. And he yanks his *pants* off. Then he drops his *drawers*. And he's hoppin' around like a fart in a fryin' pan and he's yellin' out—Okay you guys. Let's see you beat *this*. So he bends over. And right there on each cheek of his ass, he's got these twin propellers. And underneath, in red and green letters, it says Port on one side and on the other side it says Starboard. Well. We figured, you gotta admit. This guy wins the contest. But *then*. Right then is when Mc-Finlay starts to scream—You ain't seen *nothin'*. Take a look at *this!*

Cooper glanced at Whiskey Bill, turned his face to the window, shut his eyes and swallowed.

So McFinlay, he drops *his* pants. And right across his belly he's got a tattoo of a whole bunch of hound dogs runnin' to beat hell and bayin' at the moon. Which is really his belly button with a circle around it. Then he starts to turn around real slow and we're lookin' at this panorama. All the rest of these dogs are runnin' behind the side of his hip and across the cheek of his behind. And then. *Then*. There's this *rabbit!* But all you could see was his hind legs and his tail. And the rest of him is disappearin' right up McFinlay's *ass*hole. I mean it. Right up the old bunghole. You don't believe it, you ask him some-time to show you his tattoo. Oh, I'm tellin' *you*. The nuts you meet in this seagoin' profession. Jesus Christ. It's un-fuckin-believable sometimes.

Whiskey Bill chuckled, his belly jiggling, one eye closed in a tight wink as the other eyebrow made a high arch. The cab went over the elevated highway, the driver looking at his passengers in the mirror.

Hey. Youse guys Merchant Marines?

Cooper scowled at that same old tiresome error. But Whiskey Bill smirked, holding his cigarette by two fingers.

Yeah. That's us. We're regular Ancient Mariners.

Yeah? No kiddin'? Listen. What do you do on the ships?

Who, me? I'm the First Assistant Engineer.

Cooper jerked and grinned, then held his hand over his mouth as he pretended to scratch his nose. When he felt the spasms of pain behind his eyes, he winced, faced the window and licked his upper lip slowly. Whiskey Bill sat with a straight face, basking in the driver's admiration.

Yeah? That's like, whaddaya call it? Like an officer.

Oh, sure. Hell. If I was in the navy or anything like that. Oh, I don't know. I suppose I'd get a commission as a lieutenant commander. At least.

Whaddaya, don't wear your uniforms when you're on furlough. Right?

Naw. Too much trouble.

Whiskey Bill looked at Cooper and smirked.

So, anyway. Like I was sayin'. I mean like, it's a reg-ular occupational hazard. Hell. I wouldn't even be shippin' out on this bucket right now if it hadn't been for these two characters I just got tangled up with. Chico and Beef Stew Smitty. *Real* nuts. I mean, genu-wine *pistachios*. What happened was. I already had me a job, see? I was the Crew Pantryman on the *Lucius Peabody*, goin' to Spain. Man. Spain is the cheapest country in the whole world. You can go ashore with five bucks and get stewed, screwed and tattooed and still come back with change. As a matter of fact, I had myself one hell of a time just gettin' on the *Peabody* in the first place. When the job was about due to come up on the board, there was a whole mob down there. But I had the oldest Steward's Department registration card in the hall, see? Eighty-five days. The trouble was. There was this old rum-dum chief cook named Beef Stew Smitty who had a card even older'n mine. His was eighty-*seven* days old. But I wasn't just gonna give up *that* easy. What happened was. This friend of mine gives me this inside tip that they was gonna call for replacements sometime that day. And one of the jobs was gonna be for a messman. So I goes wanderin' down the street and sure enough. I sees old Beef Stew sittin' in Clancy's bar. I knew the old fuck must have been broke 'cause he was only drinkin' draft beer.

The taxi stopped at the toll plaza and then entered the tunnel under the East River, the tires and the engines of the automobiles and trucks making a reverberating roar within the tile-lined tube. Whiskey Bill raised his voice to compensate the interference, the cab driver turning his head to listen, watching the road ahead out of the corner of his eyes.

So I goes in and real casual I orders a double Scotch on the rocks. Smitty's tongue must have shot out at least three feet. So then me and him gets to talkin' about this and that and real nonchalant I mentions the *Peabody*. Sure enough. Right away I finds out that he's layin' for this Spain job and he figures that with *his* card, he's got it knocked up. Well, it was about a quarter to eleven and I had it figured that the job would come up on the eleven o'clock call. So I thinks real fast and offers to buy Beef Stew a shot. Man, I made a big production out of it. You know. Us bein' old shipmates and all that crap. So he drinks the shot and I buys him another one. A double.

Well. In two or three minutes he begins to get a slight glow on. So I starts laughin' real hard and I says—Hey, Smitty. Tell us about that time you made a trip with old Red Lead Johnson and he come down to the galley with his pistol and threatened to shoot you if you ever served beef stew for breakfast again. And so sure enough. Smitty starts tellin' us how he chased Red Lead out of the galley with a cleaver. And Red Lead, he only had a towel wrapped around his ass and this high-pressure cap on his head with all this gold braid on it. And while he's runnin' down the passageway with Smitty screamin' right behind him like a Borneo headhunter, the towel comes off, gets tangled up around his feet and he trips and falls. The pistol goes off and shoots out this overhead light and the glass comes down and makes a big cut on the cheek of his ass.

The taxi came out of the tunnel, made a sweeping turn to the left to circle around and go through the underpass to South Street. It twisted through the old and narrow streets until the driver stopped at 42 Beaver. Cooper opened the door and got out, very carefully placing the cardboard box on the seat before he followed Harrison into the lobby of the building. He pushed the elevator button and waited.

Anyway, Beef Stew is tellin' this old sea story all over again. And he starts huffin' and puffin' about what a son of a bitch Johnson is. And I'm givin' the bartender the wink and feedin' Smitty six or seven real fast shots. In about five minutes Smitty was ravin' like a madman, all carried away with his own bullshit. But while he's screamin', I slips out the door and runs down the street to the union hall. I made it just in time, too. There was a riot goin' on down there, everybody climbin' on top of each other to throw in their cards. McFinlay was callin' out that he had a card eighty days old when I comes gallopin' up like the Lone Ranger and yells out—Hold everything. I got him beat.

The elevator door opened. Three people stepped out and Cooper and Whiskey Bill Harrison stepped in. Just as the door was closing, a middle-aged man in a business suit came running into the lobby. Cooper grabbed the door and held it.

Thanks a lot, breathed the man as he entered.

What floor you want? asked Cooper.

Seven. Please.

The door closed. The elevator started to rise.

So like I was sayin'. I was tellin' you how come I was to get that job on the *Lucius Peabody*? So anyway. McFinlay there, he writes me out my shippin' ticket and I go to the company doctor and all that stuff. Naturally, it had to be this same Doctor Haiffen guy. He mentions the fact I'm a little bit overweight. But still. He gives me a fit-for-duty slip. So I grabs a taxi and—*swish*. I runs out to Brooklyn to this flop I had. I was stayin' in this room which is upstairs over this bar I know on Fourth Avenue. I been hangin' out there for years. Every time I'm on the beach. This bartender Tommy, me and him split the rent for this room and when I'm at sea, he uses it to shack up in. He's married now, see. So it comes in handy. The thing was. I was about three months behind in my half of the rent. So I comes in and gets all my gear together and drags it downstairs, around the corner and into the bar. I says so long to Tommy. I'm goin' to Spain right after we makes this coastwise trip and I'll be gone about two months. So we has a farewell drink and then I jumps into another taxi and runs out to Red Hook where they got this ship tied up.

The man in the business suit glanced at Whiskey Bill and then at Cooper. Dutifully he faced the front.

Don't forget now. This is Monday I'm talkin' about. Only three god-damn days ago. So I goes abroad and gets myself settled down in the focsle. I throws all my gear into the locker and I gets some clean linen from the Chief Steward and I'm all set. I lights up a smoke and I gets talkin' to this little Porto Rican guy named Chico who's in the same focsle with me. And he breaks out a bottle of monkey rum he's got stashed away in his locker. So we passes the bottle back and forth and Chico starts tellin' me all about the last trip the *Peabody* made. I'm tellin' you. Them guys must have went plain ape shit. Two solid weeks in Spain. Bullfights. Flamenco. Wineskins. Exhibitions at the whorehouses. Man. I could just see myself over there. Drinkin' up on all that vino. Gettin' laid, relayed and marmalade.

The elevator stopped. The door opened and the man in the suit stepped out quickly, looking back over his shoulder. The doors slowly ground shut. The elevator continued up.

So anyway. We took off the next morning to start the coastwise run to Baltimore. And the next day, just before coffee time, we tied up at Sparrow's Point. So. Just when I got done cleanin' up after lunch, I comes into the focsle and right behind me Chico comes runnin' in and says he wants me to double up. Work as Pantryman and as Messman both. And serve supper for him. He's got a real special date and he wants to go ashore early. Special date, my ass. It was one of them sloppy B-girl whores that hang around Monkey Wrench Corner. But this Chico is beggin' and pleadin' with me to do him this one big favor. And the next thing I know, he's offerin' me all kinds of money. And he's bringin' out this monkey rum again. So I figures, what the hell. I can always go ashore later. But I was still holdin' out, see? Then this Chico gets this real weird look in his eye and he says—Hey. You wanna have a little smoke? And he pulls out some cigarette papers and this tobacco sack. So I'm not narrow-minded or nothin'. A little reefer now and then never hurt nobody. So I rolls myself a smoke and I sits there inhalin' away and holdin' my breath and in a few minutes I'm way up there in the crow's nest with the rest of the birds. Finally I lets out a sigh and I says— Okay, Chico. You go shit, shave, shower and shampoo. I'll just stay home and do the dishes. Chico, he jumps up and heads for the door like a red streak from a forty-five.

The elevator stopped at the eleventh floor. They stepped out into a reception room, the thin nurse behind the desk looking away from Harrison with a hard frown, flinching when they gave her their seaman's papers and shot cards. They went into the waiting room and sat down. Cooper banged the ashes out of his pipe into a heavy tray. Whiskey Bill lit a cigarette, looking around the waiting room. Cooper relit his pipe, crossed his knees, picked up an old copy of *Life* and began to flip the pages.

So after Chico went ashore, I shut the porthole and the door and put the fan on. Then I turned off the overhead light. It was kind of stuffy in there, but I couldn't afford to let the whole crew in on the deal. So I just takes it easy, layin' back in my shorts like old Buddha. I'm communicatin' with the infinite and meditatin' on my navel. And I'm reachin' over for this rum bottle I got under my bunk and takin' a quick belt now and then. But after layin' around in there for most of the afternoon, I'm gettin' pretty well geed up. About all I needed right then was some benzedrine, some hot peppers and some Spanish fly. Well. By this time it was nearly four o'clock and I had to start settin' up the tables in the messhall and get ready to serve chow. Only trouble was, I got all the way down the passageway to the messhall when I remembered I didn't have nothin' on but my shorts. So I had to go all the way back again to get my clothes.

Whiskey Bill chuckled. Cooper tried not to grin, tightening his lips and concentrating on the magazine.

So anyway. I'm marchin' down the passageway to the focsle, see? But about halfway down I starts thinkin' I'm a paratrooper. There's about fifty of us and we're all marchin' across an airfield to this big plane that's waitin' to fly us off on another real tough combat mission. In the meantime there's a bunch of enemy planes divin' down and they're strafin' the hell out of us. And the bullets are bouncin' all over the bulkheads and the ack-ack is blastin' away. But I don't pay no attention to that stuff. I'm just marchin' along, see? And I'm goin'—hup, tup, rip, hor— And then the next thing I know, we're flyin' over our objective and I'm goin' down the aisle of this big transport plane with my static line hooked up. And this red light keeps flashin' and I'm grabbin' my parachute pack with both hands. Only it was really my belly, see? And by the time I reached my focsle I'm all ready to bail out. I give a fast, flyin' leap headfirst right through the door and all the while, I'm yellin'—*GERONIMO!* And I falls flat on my face on the deck.

The *Life* magazine lay in Cooper's lap as he held the burned-out pipe in his hand, staring at Whiskey Bill.

Man. I damn near killed myself. I'm tellin' you. When I finally managed to get my wits together, I stood up and started to look in the mirror to see if my nose was bleedin'. But I stopped myself just in time. Them mirrors can be dangerous as hell when you're all smoked up. Sometimes you can get hung up lookin' at your own reflection and thinkin' how pretty you are and you can stand there for hours just chirpin' and cacklin' away like a god-damn parakeet. Well. Eventually, I managed to find my way back to the bunk. Then I sat down and had a good long shot of rum to sort of straighten myself out. Then I got dressed and *finally* I started to feel my way to the mess-hall. But by the time I got there, the meal was already over. I runs into the Second Cook just as he comes through the door and he growls at me like he's real mean—Where the hell you been? I tried your door an hour ago and it was locked up tighter'n a clam's ass with lockjaw. He was a real sharp one, that cook was. A real comedian. Anything I hate is a god-damn comedian. But I knew I had fucked up real bad. So I didn't say nothin'. I just started cleanin' up the mess from chow.

Whiskey Bill chuckled, shutting both eyes.

Oh, Jesus. I'm tellin' you. Hey, listen. That fuckin' doctor is takin' his sweet-ass time, ain't he? I mean. We're supposed to be emergencies.

Cooper didn't answer.

So I'm there in the pantry, see? On the *Peabody?* Like I was sayin'. I fills up one of these big metal tubs with hot, soapy water and the other one with clean water and I'm sloshin' around and splashin' soapsuds all over the place and I'm rattlin' dishes and raisin' all kinds of hell with myself. Then I lights up another stick of giggle grass. So I'm in there puffin' away like a madman and I starts singin' this opera stuff. I whips through *Carmen* and knocks off a little Stout-Hearted Men and at first it seemed like I was stuck away in that god-damn pantry for hours. You know what that weed can do to your sense of time. Actually I figured maybe it was only about fifteen minutes. But I must have got hold of a late crop or somethin'. 'Cause come to find out, I *was* in there for hours. Hell. By this time it was about ten o'clock. And there I am, in soapsuds up to my ankles, a case of third-degree dishpan hands and the whole god-damn ship deserted. But man. I was havin' a *ball.*

A door on one side of the room opened, the doctor looking at a sheaf of papers through a pair of glasses riding on the very tip of his nose.

William Harrison? Mark Cooper? Come inside, please. Strip to your shorts and take off your shoes and socks.

The doctor went back inside.

He's a regular Kildare, this bird. Ain't he? Did you notice he didn't even look up from his god-damn scandal sheets? We could be a pair of purple Martians standin' here. With emerald green hard-ons. And he wouldn't even notice.

They stepped into the tiny, narrow dressing room furnished with a wooden bench and a row of coat hooks on the wall. Cooper sat down and unlaced his shoes, holding his head when he leaned over. Whiskey Bill chuckled.

Well, old buddy. I don't know what the great Doctor Haiffen is gonna say. But the way Doctor W. B. Harrison would diagnose your case is. You're *hung*.

Cooper grinned ruefully, his eyes opening wide as Harrison chuckled and unbuttoned his huge, billowing aloha shirt, pulling a pint bottle of whiskey from behind his belt.

But I got your medicine right here. A little something I snatched out of my suitcase just before I blasted off for the union hall a while ago. Thought it might come in handy.

Oh, man, breathed Cooper. I could use a slug of that.

Sure, buddy. Right after this Mister America contest.

They stripped, knocked on the inner door and stepped into the examination room. The doctor filled in a form.

Mark Cooper?

Yes, sir.

Age?

Thirty-five.

Length of sea service?

Nineteen years.

Place of birth?

Cooper hesitated. Then he said,

New York City.

What's your height?

Six-one.

Weight?

Call it two hundred.

Next of kin?

None.

None at all?

No, sir.

Quickly the doctor called off a list of diseases. In a bored voice, Cooper answered. To syphilis he said no. To gonorrhea he said yes. When asked how many times, he answered five. The doctor flipped the ear pieces of his stethoscope from around his neck up to his ears, holding the diaphragm against Cooper's chest.

Your heart seems to be alright now.

Cooper looked at him, sleepy and perplexed. The doctor touched the back of his left shoulder.

Scars disappeared, is that it?

What do you mean, Doc?

That incident in India. What was it? A jellyfish?

Cooper glanced over at the writing desk and the yellow slip of paper with a teletyped message on it. India? That was eight *years* ago. I went swimmin' when we were at anchor in Vizagapatam. I thought it was a Portuguese man-o'-war. I never did *see* it, actually. Later, though. I was readin' a book. And now I think it was a lion fish. They're poisonous as hell. All they have to do is *touch* you.

Yes? Really? Was it painful?

Like puttin' my arm on a red-hot stove. And *leavin'* it there. For an *hour*. I was out of my mind. Next day my arm was swollen and I had a wild scar later. But in six months it was gone.

Hmmmm. That's interesting. Really.

How did you know about that? What have you got? A tattletale system here? And what's this *heart* business?

Didn't you have heart trouble? In the Persian Gulf?

Heart trouble? Yeah. *Six* years ago. I was on this ship tied up to the dock in Khoramshahr for thirty days. It was a hundred and thirty every day. In the *shade*. One day I put a thermometer on top of the fidley where we were chippin' rust off the ventilators. Right in the sun. And the thermometer said a hundred and sixty-eight. So one day I felt tired. Really tired. And they sent a doctor down and he gave me some drops. Told me not to turn-to for five days. Said I had a heart thing because of the heat.

Any trouble since then?

No. It hasn't been a hundred and sixty-eight degrees since then.

The doctor rapidly filled out a form.

I won't have to give you a shot for typhoid. Tetanus and cholera. Typhus. And smallpox. You had them all less than six months ago. Your eyes are okay, aren't they? Any venereal problems now? Maybe I'd better take your blood pressure.

The doctor wrapped the cloth cuff around Cooper's bicep. He picked up the rubber bulb and rapidly squeezed it in his hand, watching the column of mercury rise in the gauge. He placed the stethoscope in the crook of Cooper's arm and loosened the bulb nut gradually.

Pressure's a little high. You been drinking?

Yeah. Quite a bit.

How long?

About eleven days.

In that case there's nothing to worry about. A little sea air will do you good. That's all. Put on your clothes.

Doctor Haiffen looked around. With one finger he pushed his glasses back up to the bridge of his nose and saw Whiskey Bill clearly for the first time, leaning against the wall, his arms crossed over his chest, his belly sagging over the top of his enormous shorts covered with very large red polka dots.

Hiya, Doc. How's it goin'?

I know *you*. Didn't I examine you *yes*terday?

Naw. It was three days ago.

Well, it certainly *seems* like yesterday.

I must still be in good shape now, Doc. You give me the works then. Left eye. Right eye. Bend over and spread your cheeks. Turn your head and cough. Skin it back and milk it down. I'm in great shape. You said so yourself.

When are you going to take off some of that weight? Your heart isn't going to take that load forever.

Aw, come on, Doc. It's only been three days.

Alright. Right now I think I'll prescribe a long ocean voyage. The *Ocean Endeavor is* going on a *long* trip. Right?

Doctor Haiffen scribbled frantically on a form.

By the way. Right after you left. Yesterday. Three days ago. Three years or whenever it was. My nurse was changing the sheet on the examination table. And she found a black widow spider underneath it. It was made of rubber. According to the autopsy I had to perform. After she went hysterical and beat it to death with one of my best proctoscopes. I don't suppose you'd know anything about the incident, would you?

A rubber *spider?* Come on, Doc. I'm forty-two years old. You think I run around playin' with kids' toys?

No. I didn't really think *that.* Alright. Harrison. The nurse will give you your papers. Outside.

Okay, Doc. Take it easy now. See you next trip.

Yes, indeed. Bye, bye, Harrison.

Cooper had already gone into the dressing room and had his shirt on when Whiskey Bill came in, grinning.

Man. I got that phoney bastard *talk*in' to himself. But wait'll he reaches into that little kit bag of his and finds that rubber *rattle*snake I planted in there just now. *Haw!*

Bill chuckled as he took down his pleated slacks from the hook on the wall and began to step into them.

Listen. Bill? That jug you got. I mean——uh——

Oh, yeah. Man. Let's celebrate. Here. After you.

Cooper's hands began to tremble as he unscrewed the cap on the bottle, raised it to his mouth, drank and shuddered.

Whewwww! Wow! I needed that. I really did.

They got their papers from the nurse who turned her head as Harrison winked. They waited for the elevator, stepped inside and faced front as the doors slid shut.

So listen. Let me finish tellin' you.

You mean there's *more?*

Hell, yes. There's more. I ain't even started yet.

Cooper rolled his eyes toward the ceiling.

Listen. I hate to freeload on a guy. But that bottle you got is pretty god-damn convenient. I mean. Do you mind?

Naw. Here, man. Have another jolt.

Whiskey Bill watched him as he tilted the bottle for a long, gurgling drink.

So anyway. Last night. Oh, jeez. It's hard to believe all this was happenin' to me only last night. I mean. There I was, washin' all these dishes. And I was washin' 'em real *good*, too. I must have spent at least a half hour on each one. Then I gets this idea of spinnin' 'em on top of the rinse water. Some of them soup bowls would spin a couple hours at least. And if one of 'em had a little chip on the edge I'd make side bets with myself which way the chip would be pointin' when it stopped. You know. Like a floatin' roulette wheel. But after that I started skippin' 'em like a flat stone on a pond. Man. I could skip them plates off that water and they'd bounce out and land right on top of the worktable. And I was practicin' hard to develop a technique so I could make 'em stack themselves in a pile. You know. Like automation. But then I fucked up. One of 'em went straight through the door and crashed on the deck in the galley. But, man. This turned out to be my biggest inspiration. Flyin' saucers. I'd give

these dishes a fast flip and, while they was spinnin'
through the air, I'm blastin' away with these ack-ack guns.

Cooper handed back the bottle. Harrison drank from
it, tucked it under his belt and covered it up with the
tail of his shirt. The elevator stopped. The doors opened.
They walked out through the lobby and across the sidewalk. Cooper's movements were more athletic and swift
as he got in the taxi, moving the cardboard box back to
his lap, wrapping his arms around it, hugging it to his
chest.

And oh, *Christ.* Them plates are really comin' down
in flames, crashin' on top of the stoves and against the
bulkheads and all over the deck. But the way it turned
out, the Captain was asleep up topside, see? And he heard
all the commotion and comes pussyfootin' down the outside ladder and sneaks around the deckhouse behind the
cargo winches by number three hatch and sticks his nose
around the edge of the galley porthole. I'm tellin' you. He
damn near got that nose of his taken clean off by the
fastest flyin' saucer ever seen. It was the flagship of the
fuckin' fleet, for Chrissake. A nice blue light comin' out
of it and these death rays shootin' in all directions. So I
yells out—Watch it, Captain! Them guys are comin' out
of that flyin' saucer and they're mad as hell. The Old Man
turned white. *They're* mad? he screams. Oh, Christ.
Could he *scream.* Seems like everywhere I go I run into
all the champion screamers.

They directed the cab driver to the Customs House
and leaned back as he began to maneuver through the
Wall Street traffic jam. Whiskey Bill lit a cigarette and
flipped the match through the window.

And the very next thing I know, he runs inside the
pantry and commences to shake his fist under my nose
and he's howlin' like a hyena—Pack your god-damn suitcase. You're fired. So I looks at him and I thinks real fast
and I says—You can't fire me. I done signed the Articles

for a foreign voyage. Less you wanna pay me a month's wages. Plus my transportation. Oh, man. When I sneaks that last one in, he lets out a *real* roar. So you're a sea-lawyer, too. Huh? Okay. How about a little matter of destroyin' ship's property? How about attempted assault of the Master of the vessel? Then he gives a couple of sniffs and he says—And how about possession of narcotics, huh? How about *that* one? You fat, stupid son of a bitch. I'll fix it so you'll never go to sea again as long as you *live*. Well. The way I figured it, he had me by the short hairs. So anyway. I finally made a deal with him to get off the ship with no more trouble if he's willin' to forget all them charges.

The cab driver jerked the taxi to a stop for a red light, turned and grinned at his passengers, snickering convulsively. Whiskey Bill frowned.

So I runs down to the focsle and quick as a bastard I throws everything into my suitcase and my seabag. But by the time I gets to the gangway, the Captain, he's already there, rarin' to go. Then I tells him that the Shipping Commissioner would be closed up that time of night. But he started rantin' and ravin' all over again. He knows the commander of the Coast Guard personally and he'll pay the Commissioner an extra week's pay right out of his *own* pocket. Anything to get rid of *me*. So we shoots up the dock, me practically runnin' to keep up with this nut. And that damn seabag is fallin' off my shoulder and the suitcase is bangin' against my knees. But by the time I gets up to the gate, the Captain's already sittin' in a phone booth, screamin'. Then he makes six or seven more calls. And he screams some more. Pretty soon a cab pulls up. And we jumps in. All the way downtown, I'm slouched down in the corner, tryin' to collect my wits. The Captain, he just sits there, chewin' his fingernails.

Cooper moved his hand in a loose gesture that simultaneously suggested, asked and prodded. Harrison reached under his shirt and pulled out the bottle, handing it to Cooper.

By this time I'm beginnin' to feel sorry for this guy. You know. Havin' to put up with assholes like me all his life. Just to sort of smooth things over, I offers to pay the cab driver. But when I open my wallet, I sees this rubber ten-dollar bill I bought one time in a joke store. Well. That did it. I looked at it for a split second, tryin' to make up my mind. Then I took it out and handed it to the driver who's sittin' there about half asleep. And I says—You got change for a ten? He says—Yeah. I can change it. So I says—Okay. But you'll have to catch it first. And I gives a real hard yank. Well. That god-damn thing must have stretched four feet before he finally lets go. When he does, it snaps back and pops the Captain right square in the mush. Well. That just about broke me all up. I never had seen that gag work so good before. I pretty near rolled on the ground. The cab driver, he just sits there, blinkin' his eyes. But the *Captain*. Oh, Christ. You should have seen *him*. His mouth was hangin' open and I could hear this grumble deep down in his throat.

The taxi turned at the end of Wall Street and went down Broadway until the driver found a vacant hack stand at the corner of Battery Park. Cooper and Harrison crossed the street and went into the Customs House. They looked at the directory, got in the elevator and went up.

Anyway. That was the end of me and the *Lucius Peabody*. Like I was sayin'. If it wasn't for that weedhound Chico I'd never have to ship out on this stupid *Ocean Endeavor* in the first place. I could have made all them real fine ports in Spain. But naturally. Everything had to get fucked up. It just *had* to.

They went into the Shipping Commissioner's office where a gray-haired man wearing a white shirt and a tie took out three copies of the Articles of Agreement for the

S.S. *Ocean Endeavor*. He straightened the carbon paper inserted between the very large sheets and laid them on top of the counter. Cooper and Harrison showed him their fit-for-duty slips and their Merchant Mariner Documents. With indelible pencil, the Commissioner quickly added their names to the list of the crew in block letters. On the same line he wrote out their Z-numbers, ratings, ages, places of birth and citizenship. Cooper verified that the address on his paper was correct; 25 South Street, the address of the Seaman's Church Institute which five other men on the ship had already given. He made no allotments. Harrison gave an address in Schenectady, New York, and made out the legal maximum allotment, payable twice a month, to Mrs. Molly Harrison, his mother.

Say? Who's the Old Man on this wagon, anyway?

The *Master* is Sven Pedersen.

*Pede*rsen? You mean Sneaky *Pete* Pedersen?

I don't know. He's just *Captain* Pedersen, to me.

They signed on. As they waited in the hall for the elevator, Whiskey Bill covered his eyes with his hand.

Oh, Jesus. What a trip *this* is gonna be.

Why? Is Pedersen *that* bad?

Bad? He's one of the snarliest, growliest, no-sense-of-humor sons of bitches in the business. I sailed with him two or three years ago on a tramp Victory. All up and down the west coast of Africa. He logged me two-for-one. *Three* times. And once he even logged me *four*-for-one. The phoney old fuck. The truth is, he had a real hard-on for me. All on account of one morning I was all juiced up and I figured the ship needed a good laugh. So I turned-to with this special tee shirt on that I got. It's black, see? With white letters on it that says, "I am an alcoholic. In case of emergency buy me a beer." The grumpy old son of a bitch. He never did recover from that one.

The elevator doors opened. They stepped in.

The trouble was. The American consul was visiting the ship that day. With his wife. And one of them native government officials. Not only that. Pedersen is *still* convinced that I'm the guy who put that artificial dog turd on top of his bunk. It was made out of plastic, see? Real shiny. And I mean it was *really* realistic. Oh, man: It was a gorgeous imitation. Big, round turds. Golden brown and curved and curled up in a pile. It was so real you could practically *smell* it.

The elevator stopped. The doors opened. The operator looked hard at Whiskey Bill as he stepped out, chuckling.

Oh, boy. Wait'll old Sneaky Pete sees *me* comin' up the gangway. The old bastard. He'll have a fuckin' *heart* attack.

The taxi driver started back to Brooklyn, going through the Battery Tunnel. Whiskey Bill and Cooper took turns at the bottle. Cooper filled his pipe, lit it and folded his arms on top of the cardboard box.

Anyway. Let me finish tellin' you. So right after I got paid off this *Peabody* scow, right away I grabs a taxi, shoots over to the station and jumps on the first train goin' back to New York. The train pulls in and I gets off at Penn Station and I jumps in a cab and—swish. I heads out to Brooklyn to Tommy's place. First I runs upstairs and dumps all my gear in the room and then I goes back down to the bar. So I comes strollin' in. I'm relaxed and casual and I says—Hello, Tommy. Whaddaya say? But Tommy, he just lets out this long moan—*Whiskey!* I thought you shipped *out!* That fuckin' Tommy. You'd think the stupid prick could at least *act* glad to see me. Anyway. I climbs up on a stool. I had a pretty good glow on at suppertime before me and that Captain started goin' round and round. But I had to sit on that stupid train like a dummy all the way up from Baltimore and by now it was about two in the morning. So I asks Tommy to fix me up about two or three ham sandwiches and I washes 'em down with some cold beer. I switched back to Scotch again and pretty soon I was beginnin' to get well.

Smoothly the driver came to a stop at the toll plaza, then resumed his speed, entering the Belt Parkway.

So there I am. And I'm lookin' around at what's goin' on. This joint Tommy has is a real bucket o' blood. Fights and music and broads runnin' in and out all the time. The cops drivin' up every couple hours. But right about then I'll be damned if this old nut Beef Stew Smitty don't come chargin' in. At that particular moment he was about as welcome as a dose of clap. And he starts howlin'—Whiskey Bill. You're a son of a bitch. You done rolled me for my job. So I growls at him somethin' or other, like—What the fuck's the matter with you? But the old bastard starts commencin' to blow his top—I know all about it. Pete the Greek was in the hall when you come gallopin' in like you was breakin' the four-minute mile. And *then*. After you beat me outta my job, you go run off and get your ass fired in two days' time. So I growls somethin' or other. Like, uh—What are you talkin' about? *Fired?* I paid off. Mutual consent. But Beef Stew Smitty, he rants and he raves and he whoops and he hollers until finally I bought him a shot just to quieten him down. He takes the shot alright. But he keeps right on howlin'. *Finally.* After about fifteen drinks, he starts to simmer down. But in the meantime there's this good-lookin' babe sittin' in the corner booth all by herself. She was makin' like she was puttin' on lipstick and all that, but I could tell that she's listenin' to what's goin' on. And I'm tellin' you. This broad had a pair of knockers on her that would knock your eyes right out of your head. So I nudges Smitty and I says—How would you like to take a bite out of one of them? But he turns around and says—Aw. They're just falsies. So I says —So's your teeth, you lyin' bastard. What would *you* have to lose?

The taxi suddenly swerved. Frantically the driver snatched at the wheel, jerking back to an alert position.

Hey, man. Take it *easy*. Anyway. Smitty starts to tell me that I don't want to fool around with that dame. Except that when I asks him why the hell not, he just swivels around on his seat and he gives me this real funny look. Then he brings his head right up close and he whispers—She's a nympho*man*iac. Well. I perks up a little when I heard that but I didn't let on none. I just picked up my drink and polished it off and ordered another round. Then I says to Smitty—How the hell do *you* know? And he says—I laid her myself, once. Well. Right away I know he was lyin'. That old goat. If he was to ever make out with a good-lookin' piece like that, there'd be a ticker-tape parade up Broadway. But Smitty, he gives me a funny look and he says—Well. Why don'tcha find out for yourself, why don'tcha? And then he buys *me* a drink. Right then I should have known there was somethin' wrong. That Beef Stew Smitty is so tight his eyeballs squeak. But you know. That broad had me too excited.

Harrison paused, pulled the bottle out of his belt, held it up to the light to check the level of the whiskey and drank. Shuddering, he passed the bottle to Cooper.

Here. You might as well kill the rest of it.

Cooper raised the bottle, hesitating to turn his head.

Yeah. So. Go on. What happened next?

Well. I gets up and goes over and real nonchalant, I starts playin' some numbers on the jukebox. But I wasn't payin' too much attention to what I was doin'. As a matter of fact, I punched one number three times. "Love and Marriage." Jesus. I thought that damn thing never *would* shut up. Anyway. I wanders over real casual to this corner booth and I asks this broad if there's any number she wants me to play. You know. I'm just friendly. So right away she says—Yeah. Play seventeen and twenty-three. So I plays the numbers on the jukebox for her and I comes waltzin' back and real polite I says—You don't mind if I join you. Do you? And she says—No. Sit down. Then we starts talkin' about this and that and I tells a few jokes and I smiles real pretty. You know. Puttin' on the old charm. And I waves over to Tommy and signals for two Scotches.

The taxi stopped in front of the main gate of the Brooklyn Army Terminal. The meter read seven dollars and thirty-five cents. Whiskey Bill gave the driver a ten-dollar bill and told him to keep the change. Cooper reminded him:

Listen. I owe you for half of that. Okay? I'll pay you back first time we get a draw.

They unloaded their gear. Cooper helped with the clumsy weight of the steamer trunk. Whiskey Bill balanced his suitcase on top and pushed it through the swinging glass doors. He went back for his seabag, the anxious cab driver standing by the open door of the luggage compartment.

Well. Have a good trip, you guys.

Cooper reached for the fancy lanyard of his seabag, wrapped it around his fist with one quick motion and swung the bag up to his shoulder. The cab driver harked his throat.

Listen. I got a cousin in the Merchant Marines. Youse guys might happen to run into him. Name is Clubar Bowkowski.

Cooper rolled his eyes with annoyance as he bent his knees to pick up his cardboard box. But Whiskey Bill paused, wrinkling his brows.

Clubar Bowkowski? Nope. Can't say I ever did.

Cooper and Harrison went inside, putting down their gear and going up to the counter where a Military Police corporal was on duty, wearing a perfectly laundered uniform with ribbons on his chest, an M.P. brassard on his arm. With a routine air, he wrote out two ID cards which they pinned to their chests with pins from an open box on the counter.

Cooper looked up at a large clock on the wall.

Damn. It's six twenty-five already.

Ha. Don't worry. They can't sail without *us*.

They went through the guardhouse. Whiskey Bill trundled the steamer trunk in front of him, balancing his suitcase, peering over the top of the load as the steel caster wheels squeaked and vibrated on the coarse surface of the road. As the jeeps, the command cars and semi-trucks roared past them, they trudged along the pedestrian safety zones carefully painted with clean yellow lines on the asphalt. Every few hundred feet they stopped. They shifted their seabags to the opposite shoulder and took up their burdens with the other hand, staggering along with bent necks and side-glancing eyes as they made their way down to the piers and the warehouses and struggled past the high, overhanging bow of a P-1 troop-ship.

So, listen. Let me tell you.

Huh? Wha'?

I was tellin' you about this broad in Tommy's joint.

Oh. Yeah.

So anyway. This guy Tommy's makin' all kinds of funny faces and scratchin' his throat and wigglin' his fingers like he just went out of his mind. I figured he was tryin' to signal me that this broad had a hollow leg. But I didn't give a damn. I knew it was gonna be worth it. Anyhow. This was some Italian broad from Brooklyn who was married to some guy over in Jersey City. She said that every once in a while she'd come over to see the family. Only she would tell the family she was gonna be in town for three days. But she would tell her husband that she was with the family for a *week*. You get it?

As they passed the far corner of Pier 2, they saw a battered, decrepit World War II Liberty tied up on the other side of the slip. Up on the bow, beneath the rust stains and the grease marks, the name OCEAN ENDEAVOR was still visible in faded white paint. They stopped and put down their loads, Cooper swearing.

Oh, *no. That* can't be it. It would be illegal to raise the American flag over a rotten scow like *that*.

Je-*sus*. Oh. Fuck *me*. What a filthy, rusty old—*Man!* What kind of a fugitive from a Lower Slobbovian bone-yard is *that* supposed to be?

Cooper sighed and swung his seabag to his shoulder.

Well. What are we gonna do? It's a ship. It floats.

Whiskey Bill followed him.

It floats? Yeah. *So* far, it floats.

● ALONG THE SIDE of the ship's hull the plates were dented and corrugated, the frames showing through the skin like the ribs of an old stray dog. Blisters of rust were bleeding down over the stained and faded dark gray paint. It was easy to see where stages had been rigged over the side at different times, certain areas chipped and scraped and primed but then forgotten as the weather got bad, as the overtime quota was used up, as the Chief Mate quit or the Bosun got fired or the crew was paid off. Each project could be identified by the different primers that had been used; Rustoleum or red lead or zinc chromate, either pure or diluted with paints of various colors. But streaks of rust were still bleeding through the irregular squares of reds, oranges and pinks, revealing the awful, terminal nature of the vessel's corrosion.

Cooper and Harrison trudged through the dank, smelly warehouse with their gear. Several forklifts were shuttling back and forth with pallets of cargo. Skillfully anticipating the movements of the scurrying machines, they walked past the stacked piles of crates, sacks, bundles, bales and barrels, the wheels of Whiskey Bill's trunk squeaking and clattering over the concrete floor. At the foot of the ship's gangway they stopped. Cooper looked up and saw the patches on the bottoms of the starboard lifeboats, the rips in the canvas covers. From the wing of the bridge a spotlight dangled loosely, its spindle rusted away, the rails along the edge of the boat deck repaired with wrappings of Fiberglas tape. Cooper grinned and started to climb the creaking, swaying gangway.

Well, Whiskey?

That god-damn Beef Stew Smitty. You wait. Just wait.

Harrison left the trunk on the dock and followed Cooper up the gangway with his other gear. They were met by a very short seaman wearing a felt hat that shielded his bright, piercing blue eyes. He leaned his forearms on the bulwark and stared at them as Cooper put down his seabag and his cardboard box.

Hey. Uh. We're the new replacements.

Ha? Vat you say?

I'm the new A.B. And this is the new Messman.

Ya? Hokay.

What have I got here? Hey. You know Chief Mate?

Ha? Chif Met? Oh, ya. He go nummer fife.

Number five hatch?

They went back and got the steamer trunk. Together they carried it up the gangway, jerking and dragging it one step at a time. Harrison went topside, looking for the Chief Steward. Cooper found the Mate back aft, checking the tension of the turnbuckles and the wire lashings on the deck cargo. He gave the Mate his shipping card, carried his gear inside the house and knocked on the door of the Bosun's room. There was a growl inside and he opened it.

Bos? I'm the new A.B.

The Bosun sat on the bench and struck a match, raising it to his cigarette, both fists held together to support the match box, the skin around the knuckles red and puckered, smooth and shiny with scar tissue, the nubs of the missing fingers heavily callused and stained with grime. When he blew out the match, Cooper saw that only the small finger still remained on one hand and only the thumb remained on the other.

You hit it lucky. You got the four-to-eight watch.

You serious? How come?

One of them things is all. Nobody else wants it. There's no overtime on this scow anyhow.

Cooper carried his gear into the four-to-eight focsle. The other A.B. was lying down, smoking. Randolph Britt was about fifty and Cooper recognized his eyes and the mouth, the twitch, the quick and anxious mannerisms of a South Street wino. Cooper opened his seabag and changed into dungarees and a denim shirt, taking out a paint-spattered white cap and slapping it against his knee to get out the wrinkles. He put it on the back of his head and tilted it low over his right ear.

Well. I guess I'm ready. Who's our Ordinary?

Johan Vytas. He's some kind of a Latvian, I guess. Can't speak English worth a damn. He's on the gang-way.

Little guy? Yeah. I couldn't get through to him at all. He's okay. You just got to learn his code is all.

There was a knock. The Bosun stuck his head inside. Okay. Fore and aft. Where's Nov Shmoz Ka Pop? Vytas? He's got the gangway watch.

Alright. So one of you guys better go take the wheel.

Cooper went up to the bridge, giving the steering wheel a full turn to the left and then to the right to keep up the hydraulic pressure in the telemotor, glancing up at the indicator to make sure the rudder came back to mid-ships. The Third Mate was nervous, taking the bell book out of his hip pocket and studying his entries, looking through the door to the starboard wing outside, where the Pilot and the Captain were talking. The Third was wearing brand-new khakis and an officer's cap, which he kept shifting up and down his forehead. Cooper could see that this was his first trip as an officer, that he wasn't young, that he had put in his sea time in the focsle before he got his license.

There was a deep roar from the wing of the bridge.

Mister *Teier!* Those replacements showed up yet?

Yes, *sir*, Captain. We're all set to go.

It's about time, god damn it. What'd they do? Stop off for a couple dozen beers on the way down from the hall?

The Third Mate grinned at Cooper. Cooper grinned back.

From the main deck could be heard the pound and the gasp of a steam winch, the squeaking of a manila line running through a snatch block, the snarling voice of the Bosun.

Hold it! *Hold* it, I said! Slack it back. Alright. Heave away a little more. Okay. Punchy! You and Charley rig up the handy billy. Whitey. Deacon. Strip off the gangway ropes.

The Captain yelled down over the wind dodger.

Bosun! Let's go fore and aft and get the hell out of here. Before some other idiot breaks his god-damn ass bone.

As the sailors drifted forward to the bow, the Pilot turned around slowly with his hands in his pockets, calculating the wind, the tide, the horsepower of the ship, her draft and trim. In a low murmur he gave his first command:

Single up, fore and aft, Mister Mate.

The Third Mate repeated the order and dashed over to the telephone, turning the crank, breathing heavily as he waited for the bow to answer:

Single up, forward.

He turned the dial, cranked the phone and repeated the order to the stern. Already the sailors had thrown one head line off the mooring bitt and slacked it away. The linesmen on the dock took the eye off the bollard and let it splash into the water. Cooper stood relaxed, his arms cradled around the spokes of the wheel, looking through the portholes and watching the men on the bow. He could see the big, ugly Bosun leaning over the bulwarks and making a circling motion with one ruined hand as a signal to the lanky old Carpenter, the windlass yammering in a great clatter and hiss as the mooring lines were hauled in and flaked down. The phone rang. The Third Mate answered it, repeated the message, leaned through the door and repeated it again:

All clear aft, Mister Pilot.

Very well. Thank you.

The Pilot hesitated, hands in his pockets.

Dead slow ahead, please.

Dead slow ahead, sir.

Mister Teier swung back the handle of the telegraph and shoved it all the way forward, the sprockets and chains whirring, the bell ringing. The engine room answered. The Third Mate looked at his watch, his lips moving as he made an entry in the bell book. The Pilot put a whistle in his mouth and blew two blasts. The forward tug answered. The water began to churn as the tug pushed its bow fender against the hull of the ship. Very slowly the ship began to move.

Twenty degrees right rudder.

Twenty degrees right rudder, sir.

Cooper turned the stiff and resisting wheel, the varnished spokes squeaking loudly. The Pilot blew his mouth whistle once. The forward tug answered. The *Ocean Endeavor* backed out of the slip, going slow astern, blowing one prolonged blast of her steam whistle as Cooper opened his mouth to relieve the heavy, vibrating pressure on his eardrums. The telephone rang. The Third Mate answered it and passed on the report to the Pilot:

All clear aft.

The ship was backed out into Bay Ridge Channel and turned until she pointed toward the Narrows. The speed was increased to half ahead. The tugs were let go and moved off, giving the traditional signal of all clear and farewell: three long blasts. Captain Pedersen gave three answering blasts. There was a short toot from a tug. And a short one from the ship.

Back aft the Second Mate lit a cigarette, one foot propped up on a mooring bitt. The sailors stood beside the port rail, watching the automobiles silently flashing by along the Shore Parkway. The Deacon glared, the muscles in his jaws flexing. Reggie grinned. As Whitey hauled down the flag, he smirked with a cynical leer, his blond mustache stretched over his wide mouth. Sanitary Sam was clumsily making up the heaving lines. Phillips scratched his head and replaced the Mobile cap made of remnants of awning canvas sewn together in a harlequin pattern.

Up forward the men were looking at the enormous towers under construction for the new Verrazzano Bridge. The wheelhouse bell began to sound in a rhythmic cadence. It was seven bells. When the telephone rang, the Chief Mate took the receiver out of the steel box, pressed the button and answered:

Bow? Very well.

The Mate replaced the phone and closed the box.

Secure the bow, Bosun. Tomorrow we'll stow the lines. Make up the rest of the gear. And wash down. Okay?

The Bosun grumbled as he turned and went aft.

How the hell am I s'posed to get all that done with just the watch on deck? You better cut loose with some O.T.

On the stern the Second Mate knocked off the gang. Just before he started to go, Whitey leered up at the punching bag which was fastened to the underside of the old gun tub left over when the ship was disarmed at the end of World War II. He hit it with a hard right cross that set the bag bouncing in a momentary syncopation with the vibrating shudder of the ship's propeller. Whitey smirked at Brooklyn as he climbed the makeshift ladder to the catwalk built over the deck cargo by the longshoremen.

Inside the wheelhouse the Pilot paced slowly back and forth, his feet silent on the rubber mat. He took the binoculars out of the felt-lined box fastened to the forward bulkhead. Looking through the porthole, he checked the channel buoys.

How are you heading now, Quartermaster?

One-eight-five, sir.

Very well. Steady as she goes.

Steady as she goes on one-eight-five.

Cooper's eyes were getting heavy. As his head began to clear, there came a sharp pain, a dryness in his mouth that yearned for yet another taste of whiskey. Then he jerked himself alert as the ship began an unexpected swing, turning the wheel, the spokes creaking.

Captain Pedersen was out on the wing, turning to look aft at the silhouetted skyscrapers of Manhattan, at the lighted windows, at the colors of the sunset gradually fading. He took another drag on the cigar and put his foot on the running light box, the leg of his khaki pants reflected with green shining through the crack of the steel door.

The ship proceeded down the channel toward the pilot station. The door to the wheelhouse opened and the eight-to-twelve A.B. came in with a tray of coffee cups.

Hey—uh—Mister Mate? I got the coffee, Mate.

Okay, Kusasavitch. Set it on the chart table over there.

The Mate put on the flashlight, holding the beam down at his feet as Kusasavitch shuffled over the deck.

I got the coffee for the Old Man.

Okay, Punchy. Thank you.

I got coffee for the Pilot, too.

Yes, yes. Very good, Punchy.

There's sugar. And milk. Everything.

Okey dokey. Fine. You did a good job.

Kusasavitch shuffled over and waited by Cooper's side as he got the ship steady on course. He put the wheel amidships and slapped the king spoke.

Steering one-fifteen. Taking a little to the right.

Aw right. One-fifteen.

Going one-one-five, Mister Pilot.

One-one-five. Thank you.

When Cooper got down to the focsle, Britt and Vytas were already there. The Ordinary took off his clothes and climbed up to his upper bunk, drawing closed the makeshift curtain, an extra bedspread rigged across a piece of quarter-inch manila line. Cooper stripped off the dirty sheets and pillowcases that had belonged to the man he replaced. Pulling off his shoes, he lay down on the bare mattress in his clothes. He shut his eyes, feeling the pitch and roll of the ship through the mattress against his back, trying not to listen to Britt's monotonous litany of complaints.

I would have paid off this rotten bucket. But with shipping so lousy, I couldn't take a chance. I went to the hall and asked around. How's shipping? I asked everybody. Wow. Terrible. So I had to hang on.

Britt adjusted his reading light and took a copy of *The Wall Street Journal* from the pile on the bunk beside him.

Oh. You just wait. The chow on here is out of this world. And the Captain's a fuckin' madman.
belly and let the *Journal* fall.

Britt glanced at Cooper, adjusted the cover over his
The whole company's a bunch of madmen. Tryin' to operate an inefficient barge like this. They should scrap 'er and be done with it. Here we go. Eight knots. That's us. Wide open with a fair wind. It'll take us two months to get to Manila. Two *months*. This ship will be a floatin' laughin' academy.

Imagine. But not only that. Just to show you what

screwballs these operators *really* are. They're routin' us the wrong god-damn *way*.

Cooper faced his watch partner on the opposite bunk. Huh? The wrong way? What do you mean?

We should go *east*. Not west. Not through Panama. *East*. It's shorter. And we wouldn't be buckin' the prevailin' winds.

Cooper closed his eyes and turned his head.

Bad food. Three men to a room. *Room?* Closet, I mean.

Britt picked up his *Journal* with a scowl as Cooper rolled over on his left side, facing the bulkhead. A fan rattled in the open porthole, its supporting bracket loose and vibrating, the oscillating mechanism broken and the guard secured to the porthole dog by a piece of wire.

Cooper rolled over on his back. His mouth sagged open. He licked his lips and swallowed. With both thumbs he pressed against the top of his eye sockets next to the bridge of his nose, wincing from the pressure. With the tips of his fingers he massaged both temples with slight rotary movements. Suddenly he raised up and swung his legs over the edge of the bunk. He dragged the cardboard box out from underneath and removed his shortwave radio. He placed it on the mattress against the bulkhead and plugged it into a socket. Very quickly he connected a copper ground wire to the metal pipe frame of the bunk. He took a pair of very large and expensive earphones out of the box and clamped them over his head, adjusting the soft, thick pads of foam rubber over his ears. He lay down again, rolling over on his side, to turn off the speaker switch, to put in the jack plug of the earphones and to adjust the volume and tuning controls. Britt lowered his *Journal* to his chest to watch the proceedings, then went on with his reading.

At 0330, Whitey knocked, unhooked the door and switched on the overhead light.

Alright. Hit the deck. The weather is fine and clear. The coffee is ready. The lookout is on the bow. Come on. Let's go.

The four-to-eight watch got dressed, went to the head, went to the messhall and had some coffee. Vytas had first wheel. Cooper had first lookout. Britt had first standby, sitting in the messhall with a copy of *Fortune* magazine. At 0455, Cooper was relieved on the bow. He had twenty minutes of standby time and then went up to the bridge to relieve Vytas, taking a cup of coffee for the Mate. The wheelhouse was totally dark except for the yellow light from the gyro repeater which reflected on Cooper's face, on his hands and on the spokes of the wheel, the repeater making a sharp click whenever there was a quarter-degree change in the ship's heading. The silhouette of the Mate moved back and forth across the portholes, across the stars and the distant running lights of another ship that they were meeting. Down below, the pistons of the reciprocating steam engine throbbed and pounded. The steering wheel creaked. The repeater clicked with an uncertain pattern of silences and rapid chatter. The clock on the bulkhead whirred and then its chime struck twice, hesitated and struck again. Cooper reached up for the handle of the lanyard and gave it a yank, the loose bight slapping up against the overhead as the small bell outside sounded with a double stroke and then a single. It was three bells. It was five-thirty in the morning.

After breakfast the four-to-eight lay in their bunks, enjoying their rest period before they turned-to on overtime at nine o'clock to clear the decks and to finish securing the gear. Sanitary Sam came into the focsle with an armload of clean linen, towels, soap and matches, whining and pouting as he tottered about the room.

You guys could help out, you know. Take your dirty linen down below. I got enough to do on Fridays. Swab out the head and shower. Swab the decks in the focsles.

And the passageways. Four focsles I gotta do. And then get clean linen. And I only get two hours to do it in.

Come on, Sam. It ain't that bad.

My name ain't *Sam*. It's *John*. John Abernathy.

Britt giggled.

Okay. Would you rather be called Sanitary John?

Sam left the room, slamming the door.

The four-to-eight went back aft, where the Bosun put them to work clearing the decks. Working rapidly, they threw all the loose pieces of old dunnage over the side, the dirty, broken boards spinning in the air, slapping on the surface of the sea and then drifting back into the foam and the turbulence of the ship's wake.

Hey, you. Nov Shmoz Ka Pop. You go back to the fantail. Huh? Dump them drums and then haul 'em back up and make the lanyards fast to the taffrail again. You capish? Huh? Get that big scoop out of the lazaret and shovel all that loose shit off the deck. You savvy? Huh?

The little Ordinary blinked and hesitated, glancing at his watch partners. Reluctant to interfere, Cooper paused, looked at the Bosun, then took Vytas by the arm and pointed aft.

Garbage. You understand garbage?

Kar-bich? Oh. Oh, *ya. Kar*-bich. Ho-kay.

The Bosun muttered and walked away.

The deck gang knocked off for coffee time at ten o'clock and then began stowing the forward mooring lines into the forepeak. A couple of men helped the Carpenter put the devil's claws on both anchor chains and twist the turnbuckles tight. Just before noon the Bosun knocked everyone off for chow. The messhall was filled all at once, the Negro Messman swiftly fetching three orders at a time from the galley. Cooper took his usual place, turning the swivel chair toward the menu chalked on the blackboard.

I'll have some beef. Well done. No gravy. And some mashed potatoes. String beans. And maybe a little corn.

Zeke started for the door, repeating aloud as he went:

Dry beef well. Spuds, beans and corn.

Someone called out.

How about a piece of pie, Mess?

One deck load. How many more?

Three men ordered pie. Four wanted coffee. Zeke stepped out into the passageway and gave his orders to the Second Cook, who served from the galley over the counter of stainless steel. Zeke returned to the messhall, holding Cooper's order and a small plate of pie in his left hand. The fingers of his right hand were spread apart to hold three orders of pie. Quickly he distributed them, moving on to the pantry. Without pausing, he drew four mugs of coffee from the urn and came back, repeating two more orders as he picked up a handful of dirty dishes, several cups and numerous pieces of silverware.

Salvador Moro worked in the pantry. He had two nicknames: Flip Flop, which imitated the slap of his leather sandals against the soles of his bare feet; Plip Plop, which imitated his Filipino accent. The Pantryman scraped the dirty plates into the garbage bucket and dumped them into the sink, tossing the silver into an old paint can with holes punched in the bottom.

Cooper finished and left the messhall, lighting his pipe. Whiskey Bill was coming up the ladder from below.

Well. If it ain't the new Bedroom Steward.

Bill grunted with a muffled snarl.

What's the matter?

I'm at sea. That's what's the matter. And it's linen day. And I been down there in that hot steel locker. Sortin' out dirty sheets. Smellin' punky feet. Stale pecker tracks. Old, worn-out fart vapors. *Ahhhhh*. And that fuckin' Old Man's gonna drive me right out of my mind.

What? Wasn't Cap'n Pedersen glad to see you again?

That old nut? He's finally cracked his shell. The crazy bastard has got a *bear*skin on top of his bunk. A fuckin' genuwine *polar* bear. Damn thing is eight feet long. The head all filled with concrete. Teeth sharpened. His dumb glass eyes starin' at me while I'm tryin' to clean up the room.

Cooper grinned.

A *polar* bear? No shit?

And I ain't never gonna get that stupid rat hide just the way he wants it. Gotta have the legs at a certain angle. The head toward the door just right. *Ahhhh.* What's the matter? he says. I'm a *sea*man. That's what's the matter. Ma*roon*ed. On a ship loaded with loonies goin' halfway 'round the world.

At one o'clock the deck gang went to work. They secured the hatches, driving wooden wedges into the cleats which tightened the batten bars around the four sides of the tarpaulins. They stowed the stern lines. They made up the boom guys. And then they began to wash down, unreeling the fire hoses and calling down to the engine room for water pressure, starting at the bow and working their way aft.

● AT 1825 HOURS the sun had just begun to set when Vytas went forward to start the lookout. He leaned on the apron and looked over the side, watching the spray rise up from the stem and the continuous swell made by the bow wave, listening to the loud hisses of the foam as it swept aft along the hull. The sea was getting dark. Twilight was beginning. Vytas raised his head and looked at the fading streaks of color in the sky just forward of the starboard beam, Venus hanging very bright just above the horizon. Then he straightened up. He shielded his eyes with the palm of his hand, concentrated, dropped his gaze deliberately and then looked again. Opening the cover of the telephone box, he jerked out the receiver and began to turn the crank violently. In a moment the Chief Mate answered.

Bridge?

Hey. Man det.

What was that, Vytas? What?

Man det. You go haf look.

Where? Which side?

Starpert site. Py sun. Him det. No cloze.

The Chief Mate replaced the telephone receiver and put the sextant he was holding back in the box on the settee.

Damn it, Cooper. Can't you guys teach that Ordinary of yours to speak some English? He says there's a dead man out there.

A *dead* man?

That's what he said. At least. That's what I think he said. Just when I'm trying to shoot my stars. Damn.

The Mate went out on the wing of the bridge to brace himself against the roll of the ship and raise the binoculars to his eyes. He stood motionless a moment and then hurriedly came back, crossing the wheelhouse, stepping into the passageway to knock on the door of the Captain's office. There was a deep grumble inside.

Captain Pedersen? Would you step out here a moment?

The door opened and the ship's Master glowered.

Can't I take a little after-dinner nap without you bangin' on my door? What's the trouble now? You lost again?

No, sir. The lookout just called, Captain. And there's a naked body out there in the water.

A *body?* Oh, shit. What next? I *ask* you?

The Captain was wearing a pair of wrinkled, dirty khaki pants rolled up past his ankles and a pair of Japanese thong sandals on his bare feet. He wore no shirt, the hair on his chest the same gray as his three-day growth of whiskers. Taking the binoculars out of the Mate's hand, he strode out on the wing, changing the focus of the eye pieces before scanning the horizon.

Yeah. It's a dead man alright. Must be from an airplane wreck. Or a yacht, maybe. No vessel in distress out here.

Shall I ring the general alarm, Captain?

Hell, no. You crazy? Everybody and his fuckin' brother will be puttin' in for overtime. No. We'll just break out the Deck Department. Then I'll call it safety-of-the-ship. They'll put in for O.T. anyway. But I'll dispute it. I ought to just keep on goin'. Can't help the poor slob now, anyway. But if I don't stop, some son of a bitch of a sea lawyer will be screamin' to the union patrolman. Dereliction of duty. Custom of the sea. All that crap. Oh, damn it all. Alright. Stop the ship.

There was no answer. The Captain roared:

Mister *Mate!*

Yes, sir?

Stop the fuckin' *ship!*

Stop the ship, sir.

Mister Delray swung the handle of the telegraph, sensing the surprise of the engineer down below as he paused, waiting for the answer, his hand nervous and impatient. Checking the indicator before looking at his watch for the time, he fumbled through the shelf over the settee until he found the bell book.

Come hard right.

Hard right, sir.

Cooper began turning the wheel, heaving against the resistance of the hydraulic fluid in the pistons.

Mister Delray?

Yes, sir?

Call the engine room and let them know what's goin' on. And you better call all hands. Who's on standby, Cooper?

Britt is, Captain.

Good. If that moron Ordinary of yours was on standby I'd call all hands myself. It'd be a lot easier than tryin' to explain what I wanted to *him.*

Vytas is a pretty good man, Cap'n. It's just that he don't speak English too good.

Yeah. Yeah. I know. Sure.

The Mate ran out on the wing, leaned over the wind dodger, fished the whistle out of his pocket and blew a long blast. The telephone rang inside the wheelhouse. Breathing heavily, the Mate ran back inside and pulled out the receiver.

Bridge? Yeah. I was just going to call you. We're

stopping to pick up a body out of the water. Yeah. A drowned corpse. So stand by. We'll probably be maneuvering.

Did you get any stars? growled the Captain.

I got two. Just before the lookout called me. I didn't have a chance to work out a fix yet.

Don't worry about it. We'll figure out where we are some other god-damn time.

Shall I rig up the not-under-command lights?

What the hell for? There's nobody else out here.

Well. What about the Rules of the Road?

Fuck the Rules of the Road. Use your head, man.

The Captain saw the standby coming out of the house onto the boat deck and yelled down:

Britt! Call all hands. Get 'em out here and *fast*. None of this fifteen-minute-preparation-period bullshit. This is an emergency. Call the Second Mate. And the Third Mate. And tell the Bosun to start preparin' number one boat for launching. You got all that?

Yes, sir, Cap'n.

Britt turned and started to run down below.

And tell everybody to put on his life jacket.

Yes, *sir*.

Again Britt started to go below.

BRITT!

Yes, sir?

Forget it. Get your ass up here. Quick.

Lowering his voice to his normal, gruff conversational level, the Captain raised the binoculars, pausing to scratch at his chest.

Cooper. When you get relieved. Go below and call all hands. Somebody told me you hold a mate's license. Is that right?

Yes, sir. But I—

Never mind. I want you in the boat. I can't trust that

Wall Street tycoon you got for a watch partner. But he can't do much harm up here. Not with the engine stopped, anyway.

Britt ran into the wheelhouse, breathing rapidly, trying to calm himself.

Yes, sir?

Take the wheel. Where I can keep an eye on you. I can't have you in the boat. You'd start rowing in the opposite god-damn direction. Just to be contrary.

Britt was embarrassed, shyly avoiding the Captain's gaze as he took the spokes of the wheel, Cooper stepping off the grating.

Aw. Cap'n Pedersen. It's not that. It's just—

Shut up. Bitchin' and moanin' all the time about going around the world the wrong way. *Jesus.*

Cooper went below. The Captain studied the corpse through the binoculars, estimating the wind, the sea, the amount of way remaining on the ship as she drifted through the water. He growled to Britt to put the rudder amidships, then stared again over the water.

In a few minutes the men began to appear on the boat deck. The Third Mate was buttoning his shirt as he came into the wheelhouse, his life jacket looped over one shoulder, his belt buckle undone. The Second Mate came up carrying his life jacket, his shoe laces untied, his chest heaving as he fought for breath.

Mister Teier? growled the Captain.

Yes, sir?

You relieve the bridge. Mister Delray? You and the Second Mate go down and help those deck monkeys swing the lifeboat out. And I want you both in the boat. You need the practice anyway. Pick out a crew. But leave a couple of men behind to stand by. And the Bosun. He can't pull an oar with those hands of his anyway.

The deck gang jerked loose the slipknots in the lashings and removed the canvas cover. They took out the strong back and passed it down. They handed the sea painter down to the main deck. The drain-plug cap was screwed on. The Bosun growled and swore at several men, who grabbed the falls at each end of the boat to pull the slack out of the tackle. The Chief Mate yelled through his cupped hands:

We're all ready, Captain.

Captain Pedersen came out on the starboard wing.

So? Swing it out! What are you waitin' for?

There was a clanking of iron and a rattle as the chains were released and fell to the deck. But they couldn't let go the keel chocks, the toggle pins being frozen with rust. Banging at them with the iron bars, the men swore and jostled each other until the handles were turned with creaking stiffness. Above them, the Captain howled:

What the hell's the holdup? Swing 'er OUT!

The inboard gripes were released. The fore and aft davits were cranked out, the boat moving ponderously overboard, swinging easily with the roll of the ship. The Bosun had a couple of men lower a Jacob's ladder over the side just as Britt shouted through the wheelhouse door:

I got no more steerageway, Cap'n. She's not answering.

Alright then. Just stand by. Leave the rudder amidships.

Midships, sir.

The Second Mate was still inside the lifeboat with Punchy and the Deacon as it was lowered away, keeping their balance by holding on to the manropes. Cooper and another A.B. let the falls run out, snubbing them with figure-eight turns on the cruciform bitts. The Chief Mate looked over the side, signaling with a revolving wave of his hand. Then he turned his head, holding up both clenched fists. Reggie, Cooper and Phillips began climbing down the Jacob's ladder toward the bobbing, pitching boat while the falls stretched and slackened with each roll of the ship. The Chief Mate followed them.

Whitey. You come along too. Vytas. You stay here.

As Cooper clambered down the swinging, jerking ladder, Whiskey Bill stood by the bulwark on the main deck waiting for him with a grin, sipping from a coffee cup. His big belly jiggled with silent laughter and then he thrust the cup under Cooper's nose.

Hi ya, sailor. Whaddayasay?

Cooper jerked his head with surprise at the smell of straight whiskey, his nostrils distending. Quickly he recovered, stared at the smirking fat man puffing elegantly on a cigarette and then eagerly took a mouthful, swallowed hard and then quickly swallowed the rest. He handed back the cup as Phillips' foot came down on his shoulder, hesitated, pulled back and dangled loosely. Cooper grimaced, his eyes shut tight, his mouth puckered before disappearing down the ladder, the rungs thumping against the hull of the ship.

The men took their places in the boat. The Chief Mate tried to ship the rudder but the jerking motion made it difficult and Cooper had to help him. The Second Mate stood in the bow. At the signal, Reggie pulled out the safety pin and turned the red handle of the automatic releasing gear. Phillips yanked the wooden toggle out of the eye of the painter. The men stood by their oars. The Second Mate pushed against the side of the ship with the boat hook.

Alright! Toss oars!

There was a rattle and a bang. The Deacon put his oar straight out over the gunwale as Reggie tried to place his oarlock into the socket. Cooper tossed his oar vertically, holding it upright between his knees and looking up to turn the blade until it was neatly fore and aft. Whitey hit

Kusasavitch in the forehead with his elbow. Phillips had his oar up at a slant, letting it rest against his shoulder.

Toss oars, I said. Come on, you guys. Please.

Sheepishly the Chief Mate glanced up at the faces of the crew who lined the bulwarks, looking down in solemn wonder. Some of them were grinning at the sailors as Whiskey Bill laughed with great hilarity.

Chinamen? Hell, no! They're Mongolians! They're as fucked up as a Mongolian fire and lifeboat drill.

Mister Delray rapped out his orders.

Okay. Let's get together now. *Out* oars!

The sailors dropped their oars and held them at the ready in a more or less horizontal position, some of them with the blades held up and down, some flat, some at an angle.

Stand by to give way! Give way together! *Heave!*

With a mighty pull the men leaned back. Reggie's oar went into the water too deep. Whitey's was too near the surface and he nearly fell backward as the blade skidded ineffectually. Oars banged together. Some men recovered for the next stroke before the others. Laughter boomed down from the main deck, punctuated by the deep guffaws of Whiskey Bill. But the lifeboat managed to claw its way over the waves, the oars going like the legs of a hysterical insect.

Come *on!* Follow the stroke oar. *He* sets the rhythm. Watch what you're doing. One! *Two!* One! *Two! Heave! Heave!*

Cooper breathed through his mouth as he pulled his oar, his back and arms moving smoothly, the blade dipping, swirling through the water, rising, turning flat for the return stroke, dipping again, his shoulders tight and straining. He kept swallowing, tasting the whiskey, his thoughts excited, remembering St. Mark's Place, remembering Cooper Union, the nervous crowd which walked

49

around him. A taxi swerved out of the traffic, its horn blasting. A man held a small red dog on a leash. Another man sat on the dirty steps of a brownstone apartment house. He remembered being drunk. He remembered not being able to remember. He could no longer hear his own scream. But he could still feel it.

Moth-*er*! I'm—your—ba-by. MOTHER!

He hugged the No Parking sign against his chest. Two little girls went by on roller skates, the steel wheels clattering over the coarse texture and the cracks of the sidewalk. He wiped his wet eyes with his fingers, leaving streaks of grime. Swaying, he fumbled inside the jacket of his suit, taking out the pint bottle, some of it spilling down his neck and chest, staining his shirt and tie.

One, *two*! One, *two*! Heave! Heave! Heave!

An old bum had been watching from the doorway of a vacant store. When he saw the bottle he flipped away a short cigarette butt and staggered over.

Hey! My friend? Friend? You really must be careful. The police, you know. Caution. That's the word. Like that little motto so advisedly printed in the very center of that yellow traffic light.

Cooper rowed and swallowed down the whiskey taste.

Friend? Is there anything? Anyone could do? To help?

There's nothin' nobody can do. My mother left me. And ran off. To let me die. Or starve. She didn't care. She didn't—even *care*. MO-*THERRRRRR*! It's ME! I came *back*.

But the floating body was farther out than the Mate had calculated and he realized that the wind was affecting it more than it was affecting the drift of the deeply laden ship.

One! *Two*! Heave! *Ho*! Come on, fellas.

Whitey began to mutter, gasping and sweating.

Damn! We got to *chase* the son of a bitch?

The boat drew ahead. The Second Mate stood up,

bracing his leg against a thwart, reaching over the gunwale with the boat hook and waiting until he got within reach.

Alright, you guys. *Oars!*

Deacon and Reggie kept on rowing. Mister Delray shouted:

Oars! Avast heaving! God damn it! *Stop!*

The boat drifted, pitching and rolling as a swell passed under it, the men twisting around to look at the dead body floating face down, the arms and legs dangling loosely in the agitation of the sea.

Boat your oars. Can you reach him, Second?

The sailors laid their oars across the thwarts with an uneven clatter. The Second Mate reached out with the boat hook, barely able to touch the corpse's back. Again he reached, the blunt hook digging into the farthest hip. Sluggishly the body rolled over. With a tight, gasping voice, the darkness concealing his expression of disgust, the Second Mate called back:

My God! It's a *woman!*

What? What? A woman?

The Chief Mate stuttered slightly, his voice alternately high-pitched and deep.

Well. Get it in. And let's get back. Come on. That's what we came out here for. We have to give the thing—her—a decent burial. At least. Does she—smell?

The Deacon leaned over the gunwale opposite the corpse and began to retch. He stared down into the black water, spat, harked, dipped his hand into the sea and wiped his face.

Cooper called forward over his shoulder, his words tense and a little hoarse:

Second? Who is it? Who *is* it? Can you identify her? Does she have any identification? A bracelet maybe? A ring or something?

Trying to control his voice, the Chief Mate spoke to the men, deliberately looking away from the Deacon.

Fellas. She doesn't feel anything. Not now. She's only an object. Those are her *remains*. Not her real self.

The Second Mate pointed to one of the oar lashings.

Cooper. Take that piece of line and try to loop it over her ankle. I'll hold her steady with the boat hook. Phillips. Get her arm. Alright. Al*right*. You don't have to touch her.

The body was surprisingly light but the men were weakened by their squeamishness, flinching, reluctant to pull it into the boat. And then the leg twisted in a loose, flopping movement, the ankle and foot slipping out of the loop of quarter-inch manila that Cooper was holding, the body falling back into the sea. Impulsively the Second Mate reached down and grabbed the corpse as Phillips wiped his hands on his shirt with a shudder of horror.

For shit's sake, you guys!

Limply the corpse floated vertically in the water, the Second Mate holding it by the hair. But despite his gruff curses, he himself turned away as he pulled the head up above the gunwale. Phillips began to tremble, pointing with a moan. The woman's eyes were wide open. A tiny smile was formed on the stiffened lips, almost coy and seductive in the dim, melodramatic beam of the ship's searchlight.

—ahhhh—*ahhhhh—ahhhhh!*

God damn it to hell. Jesus *Christ!*

Oh, fuck. What the hell kind of—

The Second Mate grimaced, his back turned to the corpse. He looked at the Chief Mate, his face in anguish. Forcing himself, he slowly turned, carefully reaching his other hand over the side to grab the body under one arm. Then he stopped. His hand squeezed the arm and shoulder. He turned and bent over, looking directly down into the dead face.

Hey. Wait. *Hold* it. She's not *real!*

The other men watched, frozen, wondering.

She's not really *dead.*

Second? Are you alright? asked Mister Delray.

Me? Hell, yes. *I'm* alright. So is she. I mean. She's not alive. She's not *real*. It's only a god-damn dummy.

Whitey stared at the Second Mate. He stood up and reached for the woman, touching it tentatively and then firmly. Others began to reach, beginning to pat and to squeeze. Whitey yelled out to the Chief Mate, his voice loud with relief and final understanding.

Hey, Mate! Here. Feel it. She ain't real. It's a doll. Made out of rubber or somethin'. That's all. I'll be a son of a bitch. It's only a fuckin' *doll*.

Mister Delray slumped over the tiller, his jaw slack.

I don't believe it. Oh, no. For God's sake. What's the Old Man going to say?

Whitey began an uproarious belly laugh.

What's he gonna *say?* Sneaky Pete Pedersen? He ain't gonna *say* nothin'. Old bears like that bastard? They just scream and howl and jump through their asshole.

Reggie helped the Second Mate pull the doll into the boat, laying it out on top of the oars with nervous hands as he muttered in fascinated disbelief.

It's a fake broad. She's a counterfeit. A *phoney*.

The sailors were laughing, punching one another on the shoulder, yelling out over the water with whoops and giggles. It was difficult to calm them down but the Chief Mate finally persuaded them to ship their oars, to give way and to reach a steady, rhythmic pull. He shifted the rudder and came about, the boat rolling heavily as it broached in the trough of the sea.

On the ship the Captain stood looking through his binoculars as he growled to the Third Mate:

Have them stupid bastards all gone nuts? They gotta go *hysterical* on me? Like a bunch of school girls? Just on account of a drowned man?

Mister Delray steered the boat up to the falls and the manropes that dipped into the sea with each clumsy, sodden roll of the ship. Two men at each end grabbed the blocks and held them next to the hooks. There was a moment of hesitation as the lifeboat pitched and surged until they were able to close the automatic releasing gear.

Mister Delray looked up, blinded by the cluster lights and the searchlight which had been shifted to train directly down on the boat. Dimly he could see the engineers, the Radio Operator and the Steward standing by the rail of the boat deck. The rest of the crew gathered along the bulwarks, staring down in silent, morbid fascination. And from out of this dazzling effulgence the voice of Captain Pedersen came booming down:

Mister *Mate?* Is that a *woman* you've got down there?

The Chief Mate squinted and shielded his eyes.

No, sir. Only a dummy. It's not a dead body after all.

The crew began to mutter. The sailors started up the Jacob's ladder. When they reached the boat deck, the Bosun had them man the falls, heaving down on the tackle with all their weight, everyone grunting, stumbling and swearing, their hands and arms reaching past each other in a thick cluster, groping for a new hold on the line. Slowly the lifeboat rose out of the sea with small, uneven jerking movements. The two mates were standing up, holding on to the manropes, the nude female image stretched out on her back, her eyes closed, lying along the side bench on a pile of oars. Laboriously the boat moved up the bulwarks where the staring crew stood watching the nude body go past them as if ascending to heaven on a creaking dumbwaiter.

When it reached the boat deck, the two mates stepped off, Mister Delray carrying the doll in his arms. The Captain came running down the ladder from the bridge, striding up with exasperation and fury, a lighted flashlight in his fist.

What's this shit all about? What *is* that thing?

Never saw anything like it in my life, Captain. It's absolutely lifelike. You'd swear it was human.

The Captain trained his flashlight on the doll's face and then down over her body, her breasts, stomach and legs and back again to her face. Silently he studied the limp dripping figure that was wetting the Mate's khaki shirt and pants. Mister Delray heard a slight wheeze as the Captain's chest suddenly inflated.

What *next?* I *ask* you? What *next?* A bunch of gas-hound performers for a crew. A school boy for Chief Mate. A boiler that's shot to hell. And *now? Now* I got toy *dolls.* Floatin' all over the Atlantic like it was a kid's fuckin' *bath*tub!

Captain Pedersen whirled and stormed over to the foot of the ladder. Then he stopped, hit the handrail with his fist and turned back toward the Mate, gesticulating wildly, the beam of the flashlight dancing crazily over the crowd of amazed sailors and the littered deck strewn with equipment, tools and snarls of rope.

Fifty bucks' worth of overtime! An hour's detention! Just to rescue a drowned *doll?* How the hell am I supposed to explain *that* to the office in New York? Huh? *How?*

The Captain ran up the ladder to the wing of the bridge, screaming as he went:

Mister TEIER!

Yes, *sir.*

Full AHEAD!

Full ahead, sir!

Hard right RUDDER!

Hard right, sir!

Britt's voice echoed within the wheelhouse as the Third Mate ran inside to jingle the telegraph. The engine room answered, the sound of the annunciator drowned out by the Captain's howl:

Come back to our course. Whatever the hell it's supposed to be. One-eight-one. How about eight-one-one? Steer nine-ninety-nine if you want to. Fuck it. Steer whatever you feel like. We ain't goin' no place important, anyway.

One-eight-one, sir.

The Third Mate's voice was meek and quiet, almost afraid to suggest that he might actually know the proper course. The Captain ran up the ladder to the flying bridge where he turned off the searchlight. Leaning over the railing, he yelled down:

Get that linoleum Lorelei out of my sight. And get the Bosun to secure the boat. Never mind stowin' things away. They can do that tomorrow. But pull in that sea painter. And douse those cluster lights hangin' over the side.

The Captain ran below to the wheelhouse.

Mister Teier? Wouldn't it be rather charming of us? Maybe even sweet? Perhaps even debonair? If we put on some fuckin' *run*nin' lights? Can't you see that it's *black* out there? Do I have to tell you *every*thing? Damn it. I can't wait until they automate these ships out here. I have to run the god-damn scow all by myself as it is.

The ship shuddered as the engine began to work up and down. Slowly she came around, wallowing in the swells and then heading south, the wind once again broad on the port bow. The speed was gradually increased to seventy rpm, the familiar creak and squeal of the hull and the engine joining the monotonous bangs and whistles of the rigging aloft. Out in the darkness large patches of foam floated by, hissing from the bow all along the rusty, scabrous hull.

● LIKE A RELUCTANT BRIDEGROOM, Mister Delray stood on the boat deck watching the sailors at work, conscious of the doll he was holding in his arms. He tried to shift her to a more nonchalant position. He flung her roughly over his shoulder but found himself embarrassed by her bare buttocks next to his face. Looping an arm around her stomach, he held her at his hip, her head, hair, arms and legs dangling straight down.

Reggie finished pulling up the sea painter and feeding it to Cooper who was in the boat, coiling it down.

Hey, Mister Mate? Is this gonna be good overtime? Breakin' us out and all? On our watch below?

I doubt it. You know how tight this company is. Besides. This would come under the heading of safety-of-the ship.

What safety? The ship wasn't in no danger.

Well. That's an expression. It covers a lot of things.

Yeah. Well. I'm gonna put in for it anyway. Then you can dispute it if you wanna. And then at the payoff we'll let the patrolman settle the beef. Okay?

Alright, Reggie. Fair enough.

Mister Delray started toward the bridge ladder to relieve the Third Mate and resume his watch. The Bosun called after him, his voice wheedling and polite.

Mister Delray?

Yes, Bos?

You don't want that doll. I mean. Can we have it?

Jeez. I don't know. The Captain sure doesn't want it. You gotta admit. We earned it. Right? Especially if we end up not gettin' any overtime for rowin' out there and makin' a rescue. Right?

What are you going to do with it?

Aw. I don't know. Just fool around.

Alright. It's yours. Here. Unless the Captain needs it. To show the Port Captain. Or anything. You know?

Okay, Mister Delray. Anytime he wants it. It's okay.

The Chief Mate went up the ladder. The Bosun held the doll up with an admiring grin as the deck gang gathered around.

Who's your girl friend, Bos?

Hey. Bosun? You hustlin' street corners now?

The Bosun held the doll in front of him, bending her arms so they covered her breasts and pubic hair. In a female falsetto he mimicked a prissy, flirtatious tease:

You boys! You're *aw*-ful. But if you promise to be nice, I'll let you take me out. We can all go down to the messhall and have a cup of coffee.

The Bosun went inside the house, swinging his hips voluptuously in lockstep with the dangling legs of the doll. The deck gang jostled and pushed behind him through the passageway and down the ladder. There was already a crowd in the messhall, which greeted the doll with a spontaneous roar of wolf whistles, guffaws, groans, repeated woo-woo's and oo-la-la's. Shouldering his way inside, the Bosun stretched her out tenderly on one of the tables. The crowd pressed close, overawed, the voices reduced to respectful murmurs which diminished to a prolonged silence that was finally broken by a harsh whisper from Sanitary Sam.

What is it? What's it for?

Whiskey Bill chuckled, glancing around at the astonished faces and the ogling eyes.

What's any woman for? She's for fucking.

There was a titter in the crowd, strained and strangled.

What's the matter with you guys? Ain'tcha never

gone shoppin' around Yokohama? Just stop at the first bar and that's it, huh? Man. What worldwide travelers. There. Look at the bottom of her foot. See there? *Sailor's Friend. Made in Japan.*

The crowd tried to look over and around each other, the closest man stooping down to read the small rubber label attached to the arch of her left foot.

They sell these things in them sex shops. Man. They got dirty pictures. Stag movies. Dildos. French ticklers. It's like a regular department store. And it's legal and everything. But what you do with this doll is. The navel there comes right out. It unscrews. What you do, is. You heat up some water. Like in a percolator. You pour it in the hole and then screw back the belly button. See? It works like a hot water bottle. I mean. You don't want to go to bed with a cold-ass broad. Right?

Whiskey Bill smirked at the crowd, his belly jiggling up and down. No one moved except to glance at one another, afraid he was being conned and kidded into making himself ridiculous.

Whitey stepped closer, bending over the doll with a leer.

Jesus. What are you guys? Afraid of it?

Whitey poked at the doll's navel, twisted it, his fingers moving quickly as it began to unscrew. He held it up and then bent down to look into the hole, squinting one eye.

Yoo hoo! Anybody home in there?

Hey, Whitey? You yodelin' in the canyon already?

No, wise guy. I just wanna see if maybe she's pregnant or somethin'. With a baby kewpie doll.

Whiskey Bill continued, holding up a cigarette in a debonair pose, glancing at the pushing crowd.

Sure. Them Japs got the whole pussy problem licked. Invest in one of these and you could save yourself a *fortune* in whores.

Reggie giggled.

Hey. Where's that guy Britt?

He's up on the wheel.

Jeez. This is the company he should be buyin' stock in. Instead of railroads and telephones. They could even develop a portable model. One that you could put in a suitcase.

Somebody cackled.

Aw. Come on. You couldn't get it to fit in a *suit*case.

Sure you could. Easy. All you got to do is cut off the arms and legs. Just use the body. Like, you know. The Thrifty Thalidomide Travelin' Companion.

There was a sudden big burst of laughter in the mess-hall, all the embarrassment gone. Instead, there was a constant, competitive yelling to be heard, everyone on the ship who wasn't on watch jammed in shoulder to shoulder, the entire mass shifting back and forth as the ship rolled with a smooth, tender motion. Smiling sarcastically, amused by his own cynicism, Whitey began to sing in a clear, romantic, baritone voice:

> *Won't you be*
> *My tranquil-izer, ba-by?*
> *Cuddle up and don't turn blue.*
> *Put your stumps into my ears*
> *And let me lick your tears*
> *And I will be*
> *An amputee to you-OOUU!*

Whiskey Bill was thoroughly enjoying his role as lecturer, doctor, sidewalk barker and pimp. He looked at one man and then at another, his huge belly jiggling as he chuckled.

Yeah, man. I'm tellin' you. Them Japs can imitate *any*thing. All you gotta do is fill her up with hot water and stick in a little vaseline. And you're all set.

Hold it! *Hold* it! yelled the Bosun. You mean she's got a real *pussy?*

Hell, yes. That's the best part. It's as real as they

come. Hair. The little boy in the boat. Everything but a period. Go ahead. Take a look. Don't be scared. Spread her legs and see for yourself. It ain't got teeth or anything. It won't bite.

Whitey leered, his large wide mouth spread in a challenging grin. He rubbed his thick blond mustache with two strokes of his thumb and absently pulled at the West Coast cap that he wore, pulled low over his right ear, a pompadour of hair pushed up by the bill.

Hey. Sanitary Sam has got clean fingers. Here, Sam.

Whitey grabbed the Ordinary's hand and pulled it toward the thighs of the doll. Sam extended one finger and meekly allowed it to be inserted, his face a brilliant red as the crew let out a loud, united, exploding guffaw followed by a series of catcalls, whistles and cheers. The crew flopped in chairs, leaned on each other, those nearest the doors stepping outside for fresh air and relief. Reggie put one hand over his eyes and beat his fist against the bulkhead. The Bosun forced a grin, glancing with suspicion at the men around him as he slid both of his maimed hands into his pockets. Chips puckered his mouth in a tight button to keep from losing his chew of Red Mule tobacco. Cooper tried in vain to light his pipe, breaking up in laughter every time he struck a match. Phillips stamped one foot on the deck, turning round and round.

Leering, Whitey took Sanitary Sam's hand and raised it up in the air, the middle finger still extended as the hilarity went on for several minutes.

Listen. Now that Sanitary Sam has finished playin' stinky finger. Let's *do* somethin'. I mean. Like, who's gonna be first in the sack?

What about you, Whitey. You're supposed to be the Great Lover on this ship.

Okay, Cooper. *Okay*. You want me to go first? Fine. It'll be a pleasure.

The twelve-to-four Fireman took the stem and basket out of one of the percolators, dumped the old coffee into the sink, washed it out and filled the pot with hot water from the urn. It was passed from hand to hand through the crowd, everyone watching with profound concentration as Whitey poured the water into the doll's bladder and carefully replaced the navel. When he picked the doll up from the table her lids opened, her clear blue eyes staring at the enchanted crew.

Christ. She's still soakin' wet. Her snatch is probably loaded with sea water. Maybe got a couple of crabs in there. But I mean *real* crabs.

Whitey slung the doll over his shoulder, her long hair hanging down, her arms flopping loosely. The crowd stumbled back as Whitey went out of the messhall and through the thwartship passageway, gathering outside the open door of his focsle as he threw her down on his bunk and began to undress.

Okay, Cynthia darlin'. Just try to be patient.

The crew waited in silence, grinning with bewildered expressions as Whitey stripped, wrapped a towel around his waist and stuck his feet in a pair of wooden shower clogs. Leering at his audience, Whitey took another towel and wrapped it around the doll like a sarong. He picked her up and pushed his way through the passageway to the Deck Department shower.

The crew waited. They smoked and fidgeted, leaning against the bulkheads for support against the roll of the ship. They heard the sounds of splashing water. Wisps of steam came through the interstices of the emergency escape panel at the bottom of the door. The shower stopped. There was the clatter of wooden clogs, a low whistling. And then the door opened, Whitey standing there holding the doll in his arms.

Everyone followed him back to his focsle, but suddenly he leaped inside, unhooked the door and slammed it shut. The key clicked in the lock. Just then the ship took an unexpected roll, the men stumbling against each other as they ran for the storm door, bumping and struggling to get over the sea step and outside to run aft and shove and push for a position where they could look through the porthole and watch Whitey hug the naked doll to his chest. There were grunts and moans. The men were panting with suppressed giggles and trembling eagerness, no one noticing that the wind had been steadily increasing, that whitecaps glinted out in the darkness, that the air was filled with spray.

Whitey could see the shifting blobs of faces outside the porthole as he gave the doll a long, passionate kiss. Supporting her weight with his right arm, his left hand moved over her buttocks in slow, caressing movements, moving up and over her hips to fondle her right breast. He paused and grinned broadly toward the porthole. But then he unhooked the deadlight and dropped it over the glass, flipping a dog into place and screwing it down. There was an uproar outside and then a sudden howl. The ship gave a hard lurch, rolled heavily to port and swiftly back to starboard, meeting an unusually large sea which curled over the bulwarks just forward of the house and came washing aft with a sizzling roar and a hard slap against the bulkhead.

Some of the men braced themselves, in water up to their knees. Others were thrown. One slipped and fell flat on the deck. Almost instantly the water began to run through the scuppers, heavy rivulets splashing over the side, the men trampling and pushing each other as they stampeded back to the storm door, the last ones slamming it shut and dogging it down, water sloshing back and forth in the passageway.

Some of the men went to their rooms for towels and dry clothes. Others waited in front of the twelve-to-four focsle just as they were, disheveled and wet, their shoes squishing with sea water, impatient for the revelation.

Whitey unlocked the door and opened it. He stood

there in a towel and shower clogs, his hair unkempt, grinning, clutching the doll under one arm.

Man. This Cynthia is really hot stuff.

Cynthia? Whattaya mean, Cynthia?

That's what the slut's name is. See here?

Whitey pointed to the makeshift tattoo that he had made on the doll's left shoulder, going over and over the inscription with a ball point pen, "Cynthia" neatly lettered and encompassed by a simple heart.

The Bosun was furious.

Hey! What'd you do that for? You got no right to mark her up like that. That's like defacin' public property. Besides. We might want to name her somethin' else.

Like what?

Like. Valerie, maybe. I don't know. Anything.

Yeah? Well. Since I had to be the one to break this little mermaid's cherry, I figure I got the right to name her Cynthia. After a whore I once knew that worked on Post Office Street. In Galveston. One of the sweetest, juiciest whores there ever was. Me. I even went and married the bitch. So. Cynthia it's gonna be. Okay? Now. Who's next? Anybody else want a chance?

Reggie was chewing on his fingernails, his eyes rolling.

Hey? You didn't really screw that thing. Did you?

Christ. What do I hafta do? Knock her up? Huh? So come on. We got any more volunteers?

Plip Plop spoke up with a wide grin, two solid gold teeth prominent in the front of his mouth:

Gib 'er to me. Me peel 'er up and puck 'er good.

Phillips interrupted with sudden hot anger:

Oh, no. None of that shit. This is strictly the property of the deck gang. Ain't that right, Bosun?

There was a roar of protest and commotion, the voice of Zeke, the Negro Messman, shrill and rising still higher, furious and determined:

What is this shit, Mistuh Charley? Some mo' of yore gawd-dam' Mobile democracy?

Phillips raised his hand as he shook his head in patient righteousness.

It's only fair, that's all. We had to go an' risk our cotton-pickin' necks. Launch a boat on the high seas. Row all over the gawd-dam' ocean. Now ain't that right? So? Why should we have to share with all you Stupid Department guys?

Zeke clenched his fist and shook it.

Whut you really mean is. You don't wont no black dicks stuck in that lily-white, saint-mothuh-of-gawd-pussy.

Phillips spoke through compressed lips.

Whut ah really mean is whut ah say. Ever' time there's a boat drill. Once a week since the Merchant Marine was invented. Who's been goofin' off? Huh? And who-all's been doin' all the work? Huh? The sailors. That's who. But this time we fooled all you lazy bastards. So ah ain't in favor of you, Plip Plop or any other swingin' dick cuttin' theirselves in on the deal.

The Bosun joined the argument.

Phillips is right. We rescued her. So we keep her. The sailors all get to take turns. But nobody else. If somebody had volunteered, it might have been different.

Whiskey Bill broke in with a tight, incredulous croak:
Volun*teers*? Nobody said nothin' about volun*teers*.

Well. That comes under the heading of Tough Shit.

Whiskey Bill glared at Whitey as the Bosun yelled out:

So look. Let's start up forward and work our way aft. Chips? How about it? You wanna give her a whirl?

The old Carpenter shifted his quid, slumped his shoulders and looked up from under his bushy brows.

Are you kiddin'? I ain't had a hard-on in twenty years. If I ever do get it up again, I'm gonna dip it in varnish.

Aw, come on, Chips. Give the girl a break.

65

Nope. You want her fucked. Go fuck her yourself.

Zeke broke in again, both fists over his head:

See? See? Like ah said. You white mothuhs jes usin' that lifeboat volunteers jazz as a excuse. Chips didn't go out in no boat. Neither did you, Bosun. But you willin' to take your chance quick enough. Right? Well. Ain' that right?

Look, Zeke. Don't try to throw your weight around on *this* ship. Okay? Chips wants to pass. So I'm next. Okay, Whitey. I'll take her from here.

Sure, Bos. She's all yours. Cynthia's her name. She's a three-way girl and fun is her game.

The Bosun took the doll but hesitated.

Hey. Wait a minute. Don't you think you ought to douche her out when you're finished?

Whatta we got now? Rules and regulations? Al*ready*?

You don't expect me to take sloppy seconds, do you? Come on. Douche her out good. And comb her hair a little bit. So she'll be presentable for the next guy.

Nothin' doin'. I'll give her a douche. But that's all.

That's the trouble with guys that go to the sea these days. No consideration for nobody else.

Listen, Bosun. Never mind the bullshit. You do what you want. Comb her. Simonize her. Polish her god-damn ass. But what *I* do with her is *my* business.

Okay. So clean her up and let me have my turn.

The Bosun followed Whitey to the shower, waited for him to finish and then took Cynthia in his arms, carrying her to the room he shared with the Carpenter. Glowering at the crew still gathered in a sullen knot in the passageway, he reached up for the key hidden on an overhead beam, went inside, closed the door and locked it.

● COOPER carried a cup of coffee up the ladder to the bridge deck, balancing it against the roll of the ship as he grasped the rail with his free hand. He opened the door to the wheelhouse, moving through the dark room with slow, shuffling steps. Speaking to the darkness in general, he flinched when the Chief Mate turned on a flashlight close by.

Mister Mate?

Yeah, Cooper. Right here.

Cooper shuffled over to the wheel.

Listen, Britt. I'm late. I couldn't help it. I had to go out in the lifeboat. Did the Mate tell you?

Cooper's voice fell to a confidential murmur.

We found a sex doll out there. Whitey tried it out. He says she's hot stuff. Our turn is next. After the Bosun.

A doll? What do you mean, our turn is next?

Never mind. We'll talk about it later.

Britt went below to the messhall, lighting a cigarette, crossing his legs and watching the perpetual pinochle game. The Bosun came in. With a secretive smirk, he beckoned from the door.

Hey. Did Cooper tell you? You guys on the four-to-eight are next in line. Pass her on to the twelve-to-four.

Listen, Bos? What's this all about? Cooper was rantin' and ravin' somethin' about a sick doll.

A *sex* doll. It's Japanese. Come on. I'll show you.

The Bosun took Britt to his room where Cynthia was laid out on Cooper's bunk with a strong, sweet smell of after-shaving lotion, her hands folded over her belly, her eyes closed, her hair combed and neatly arranged on the pillow. Britt stood there. Glancing quickly at the grinning Bosun, he stared down at the doll, his voice husky and incredulous, enchanted by the miracle of this gentle, nude feminine presence which had suddenly appeared in the fetid steel room jammed with lockers, sea boots, soiled towels, disarrayed bunks, suitcases, slickers, a bench piled high with work clothes.

My God! They found *this?* In the middle of the *ocean?*

Listen. Don't blame me for that tattoo on her shoulder. That bastard Whitey did it. Like he's just *got* to make her into a cheap Texas whore. Like that wife he's got.

Christ. How is Cooper and me ever goin' to explain *this* to that dumb-ass Latvian? He doesn't understand English even when we tell him *simple* stuff.

Listen, Britt. Better keep your door closed. Them headhunters in the Steward's Department have got their nose out of joint already.

After the four-to-eight was relieved, Vytas and Britt were lying in their bunks. They squirmed and waited, turning their heads to peek at the doll, rubbing themselves, their legs shifting under the sheets with sensuous movements. Cooper came back to the focsle, a wet towel wrapped around his waist, his skin still damp and pink and smelling of Lifebuoy soap. He grinned at his watch partners, looked down at the doll, delicately pinched the nipple of her breast and tickled her vagina with his forefinger.

Ready in a minute, doll-baby.

Cooper rummaged in his locker for his toothpaste and brush, his comb and shaving gear. Hanging a dry towel around his neck, he returned to the head. Britt and Vytas waited, restless, turning their backs on the doll to stare at the bulkhead and then rolling over to verify her reality once again. Cooper returned and put his gear away. His face was smooth, his hair shining and carefully combed.

He sat on the edge of the bunk. With one motion he lay down and pulled across the spare bedspread fastened to a piece of line with safety pins. The curtain vibrated from the motion of his shifting body, fluttering slightly from the wind of the porthole fan.

There was a pause. The bunk springs suddenly squeaked and Cooper yanked back the bedspread, slipping his feet into sandals and wrapping a towel around his middle. In a moment he returned, carrying a glass half full of water from the scuttlebutt. He went to his locker and got out a bottle of Aqua Velva shaving lotion, grinning at his watch partners as he repeatedly shook several dashes into the water until it turned a very pale green.

Man's gotta have a little drink of *something*. Just to get him in the right romantic mood. Even if it is only a shaving-lotion cocktail.

Britt snickered. Cooper smiled in his direction, holding up the water glass in a toasted salute. He drank, his face breaking up into a frightful mask of squinched wrinkles and puckered frowns.

Wow. What bouquet. Whewww! Really smooth.

Cooper sat on the edge of his bunk. He turned on his radio, put the earphones over his head and adjusted several dials. Exchanging grins with Britt and Vytas, he held up his glass again and took another drink. Carefully he lay down, pulling the bedspread closed.

Britt and Vytas couldn't hear the private music coming from Radio Habana, the South American merengue playing softly into Cooper's ears. All they could hear was a few squeaks of the bunk springs, a slight sucking noise, the crack of a knee joint. His hand appeared at the bottom of the curtain, set the empty glass on the deck and withdrew. The springs squeaked more violently. They could hear Cooper's quickened breath and then a series of gasps, a single suppressed moan. There was a silence, a long grunt, a relieved sigh.

Cooper pulled back the bedspread and swung his legs over the edge of his bed, sitting there naked, his penis limp, the head enlarged and sticky wet.

Wowee! Whitey was right. She *is* hot stuff.

Britt began to giggle. Vytas raised himself on his elbow as Cooper wrapped a towel around his waist, hooked the door open, picked the doll up in his arms and went to the shower. In a few minutes he was back. He tossed the doll on top of Britt, who tittered and squirmed away from the touch of her body.

Okay, lover. She's all yours.

Britt lay still, drawn back against the bulkhead. Vytas lay on his stomach, his head hanging over the edge, staring down. Cooper made a kissing noise with his lips and drew the bedspread across Britt's bunk. Vytas rolled over on his back, staring up at the overhead. Cooper lay down, beginning to read a two-year-old *True* magazine which he had found in the spare gear locker, which was used for a ship's library. There was a titter from behind the curtain and then a muttered humming. Cooper put down the magazine and turned his head. Vytas was on his side, propped up by his elbow, trying to look down between the curtain and the frame of the bunk. Cooper winked. Vytas scowled and fell back, slamming himself hard on the mattress. And then the singing began, muted at first, but then bolder, Britt's voice hoarse and cracked and off-pitch.

> *They asked me how I knew—*
> *My true love was true—*

There were more snatches of song. A knee banged against the frame of the bunk, an elbow clunked against the bulkhead.

> *—something here inside,*
> *tells me that I know-ww—*

Vytas raised up, scowling, looking down and muttering.

Hey! Vat you tink? You no chennelman? You mak luf lak dok? You dok? *Ha?* Shaddap you. No sink dirty stoff.

Leave him alone, Vytas. It's his turn.

Vat you tink? I no slip? Sink dirty stoff all night?

Vytas slammed himself back on the mattress and grunted. In a few minutes it was quiet. Britt stuck his head out beneath the curtain. Humming softly, he picked up his dungarees from the deck, pulled them on, stuck his feet in a pair of shower clogs, reached behind him for the doll and left the focsle, his feet clattering in the passageway.

When Britt returned, Vytas was sitting on the bench in his shorts, his arms crossed over his chest. Without a word, he got up and snatched away the doll. From his locker he took out an old bathrobe with gray and maroon vertical stripes. Glaring at his two watch partners, he put it on the doll, crossing the lapels over her breasts and tieing a square knot in the cloth belt. Britt and Cooper looked at him owlishly as Vytas arranged the covers of his bed, folding them back neatly, laying Cynthia down very carefully before climbing up beside her. Pulling his makeshift curtain closed, he reached up and turned off the reading light.

Cooper grinned at Britt as he quietly closed the door and turned out the overhead light. He lay down, listening to the squeaking noises inside the insulated bulkheads, the clatter of the porthole fan, the creak and the groan of the ship as she pitched and rolled, the steady up-and-down pulsing of the engine.

He reached for the earphones, clamped them over his head and turned on the radio. Adjusting the tuning dial, he rolled over on his side, pulling the sheet and bedspread up to his neck. He lay there without moving, breathing easily, lulled and soothed by the high-pitched, quavering voice of an Arabic singer being broadcast from Beirut.

● BY SATURDAY MORNING the *Ocean Endeavor* was abeam of Cape Hatteras. The waves had built up into a short, high swell as the Gulf Stream met the tidal currents of Chesapeake Bay, the seas aggravated by force-five winds coming out of the northeast. The Captain spent the whole morning on the bridge. Glumly he leaned on the table in the chart room, reading the weather reports that the Radio Operator had filed in a paper clip hanging on a screw. He went into the wheelhouse to check the barometer. Scratching at his three-day growth of whiskers, he went out on the wing, looking up at the sky as he puffed on his cigar. The bow pitched heavily and at times there was a pounding explosion of spray, a prolonged vibration shuddering through the entire hull. The rigging squealed and whistled and moaned and the bull chain and the topping lift bail of one of the cargo booms banged continuously against a ventilator.

As the weather deteriorated, the crew became quiet and then drowsy and then sullen. They stood their watches, ate their meals and went right to their bunks, sliding up and down their mattresses with every roll of the ship. To take a shower, a man had to brace his back against a bulkhead. The spray from the nozzle would hit him in the face, but as the ship rolled it would slowly move down his body to his feet. The water would hesitate, then slowly move back up his legs and belly and chest until it hit him in the face again.

Before setting up for lunch, Zeke wet the tablecloths so the dampness would keep objects from sliding off. But when Sanitary Sam left out a jar of jelly instead of putting it back in the wooden rack, the jelly went flying off to smash against a radiator. Coffee was always getting spilled. The plates were always clattering in the sink and on the shelves. A cup was broken and then a glass. But Zeke would quickly bend down with a foxtail brush and a dustpan and scoop up the pieces, dumping them in the garbage can. He would go to the galley and return with a bowl of soup in each hand, his fingers expert as he balanced himself against the last, lurching roll, waited for the right moment and then set the bowls down. But to eat the soup a man had to be equally acrobatic, tilting the bowl constantly back and forth with one hand.

Punchy went up to relieve the wheel. Feeling his way through the dark wheelhouse, he went out the open door on the lee side. Dimly he could make out Mister Teier's figure as he leaned over the wind dodger and vomited. Punchy waited as the Third Mate whooped and gasped, coughed and retched, and then softly he called out over the moan and the roar of the wind.

Mister Teier? Sir? How about if I run down below and get you some dry bread? It'll be good for your stomach. You know. I mean. You get the dry heaves and it's gonna *hurt*.

The Third Mate harked and spat. He straightened up and wiped his eyes with the knuckle of his first finger.

No thanks, Punchy. I'll be alright.

He braced himself against the flying bridge stanchion, wiping his hands on his pants. He sipped his coffee, his throat sore and raw from the acids of his stomach. Just as he went inside the wheelhouse to get out of the wind, the Captain growled from somewhere in the darkness.

What the hell's the matter with you, Teier?

Huh? Uh. Seasick, Cap'n.

*Sea*sick? You sure you ain't *booze*-sick?

No, sir. Just plain seasick.

Don't try to tell me you don't drink.

No, sir. I drink. But not like that.

How long you been goin' to sea, anyway?

Six years.

And you *still* get seasick? Ahhh. It's all in your mind. Punchy interrupted.

No, sir. It ain't in your *mind*. It's like you get dizzy. Real bad. And then you puke. Like your balance is all outta whack. Besides. Lord Nelson used to get seasick all the time. So did Captain Hornblower.

*Horn*blower? Ain't we got enough fictional characters on this Cucamonga kayak? Who's next? Popeye the Sailor?

The Captain paced the wheelhouse, puffing on his cigar and growling to himself. He opened the door, went out and closed it. In a moment the door to his room slammed hard.

Mister Teier finished his coffee.

Punchy? Listen. Thanks, huh?

For what? Thanks for what, Mister Mate?

You know. Stickin' up for me.

Awwww. It was nothin'.

How about letting me take the wheel a minute and you go below and get me that bread. Huh? I could use it.

The *Ocean Endeavor* rolled and pitched and pounded, a short, heavy swell hitting the ship just aft of the port beam. Throughout the night the watches relieved each other, Britt coming up at the last possible moment to take the wheel just as the Deacon was ringing eight bells.

The Deacon was the last one to get relieved. He went below, opened the door and found Whitey dancing around the focsle with Cynthia, her legs dangling loosely as Reggie sat on his bunk, playing the "Tennessee Waltz" on a comb backed by a piece of paper. Whitey was stark naked. His shower clogs kept clacking on the composition deck as he spun around and around, his knees bending and flexing to keep his balance against the violent roll of the ship.

So whattayasay, Deacon? Wanna take a crack at our girl?

Aw. I don't know. Whose turn is it?

It's either you or Reggie.

Oh. Let Reggie have her. I'm tired.

A beautiful hunk of tail like this? And you're *tired?* Well. Okay. So you're tired. Here, Reggie. Give her hell.

Naw. You first. I wanna see a real pro in action.

The Deacon took a towel off the manila line stretched across his bunk. He opened his locker and took out some toothpaste and a brush, trying not to stare at Whitey's nudity as he left the room and went to the head.

When he had finished brushing his teeth, he stepped outside into the passageway. It was empty, the doors all closed. Returning to one of the stalls, he dropped his pants and sat down on the toilet. Reaching inside the crotch of his jockey shorts, he took out the wad of toilet paper, inspected the stains and dropped the wad between his thighs into the bowl. He spread his feet apart and grabbed the handrail fastened to the bulkhead. He put his other hand against the steel partition. Stiffening, he began to urinate a few drops, a hesitant trickle and finally a steady stream.

He relaxed, his face sagging, his eyes closed. Gently he dried the head of his penis with a piece of toilet paper. Then he unrolled a fathom more, measuring it twice from the tips of his fingers to the center of his chest before tearing it off the roll. Folding each square along the perforated lines, he put the new pad into the crotch of his shorts, standing up and pulling them over his hips. He picked up his pants and fastened the fly. Flushing the toilet, he turned to the sink, washing his hands very thoroughly before returning to the focsle.

Reggie was still sitting cross-legged, playing "Bell-Bottom Trousers" on the harmonica-comb. Whitey was in the lower bunk, mounted on the doll, resting on his knees as he grunted and swore in a long, continuous, incoherent groan, Cynthia's thighs up against his chest, her feet flopping over his shoulders.

Come on, bitch. Put out. Like you're s'posed to. Your daddy's got yuh, now. It's your *dad*dy. Damn your ass. *Come!*

The Deacon put away the toothpaste. He hung up the towel. He sat down and undressed, putting his shoes neatly together under the bench and hanging his pants on the frame of his bunk. He opened his locker again to take out a leather-bound Bible and clambered up to the top bunk. He took a cigarette out of the crushed pack under his pillow. He lit it, covered himself with the top sheet, drew up his knees and opened the Bible to the place he had marked. But his attention wavered. In spite of himself, he listened to Whitey's snarls and growls. And in spite of the pain, he got an erection.

Reggie squirmed and hopped, playing the tune faster and faster until he began laughing and fell over on his side. The Deacon closed the book.

Hey. Cut out the racket, huh?

Oh, man. Whitey's just makin' out. That's all.

He don't have to wake up the whole ship.

Nobody ever worries about wakin' up the twelve-to-four. Do they? Bangin' around and yellin' every mornin'?

Whitey began a low-pitched groan, his legs straight and stiff, biting hard on Cynthia's shoulder as her face turned toward Reggie, smiling with closed eyes.

There was a long pause. Reggie waited. The Deacon smoked and looked up at the overhead, listening to some loose object banging inside one of the metal lockers with every roll of the ship. Slowly Whitey let out his breath, swung his legs over the side and sat up, bending his neck forward to duck under the frame of the bunk above him.

Whewww! Baby-doll! You're sure as hell gonna be the death of *some*body.

Wow! So that's the way you do it? Huh, Whitey? None of that sweet and romantic bullshit. Right?

Just be your own rotten self, kid. They love it.

Whitey twisted around, jerking Cynthia out of his bunk, slapping her in the face with two quick, vicious blows and throwing her on the deck.

Okay, whore. Scram. You're through. Beat it.

Hey, Whitey! You're gonna clean her up, ain't you?

Ah. I don't want nothin' to do with the dirty slut.

But that ain't fair. Come on.

Aw. Wait a while. Let me have a smoke first.

Yeah. But come on. I'm horny.

Jerking up on his elbow, the Deacon leaned over the edge of his bed, muttering bitterly:

Now I suppose *you're* gonna scream and holler?

So? What if I do?

Okay. So go ahead. But I'm gettin' out of here.

Stick around. Hell. You're next.

The Deacon climbed down, pulled on his pants and stuck his feet into a pair of sandals. He went out and shut the door. His hand passed under his crotch, checking the position of the wad of toilet paper as he went to the mess-hall. It was 0425. Cooper was on standby, smoking a pipe and reading a book. The Deacon poured himself some coffee, filling half the cup with canned milk and adding three sugars.

Cooper looked up.

What's the matter, Deacon? Can't sleep?

Naw. Them two nuts I got in there.

Cooper looked back at his book. The Deacon took a drag on a fresh cigarette, his eyelids half closed, listening to the internal voice of his own thoughts.

Naturally. Sure. With my luck, guess who's gonna be the one to end up with a *permanent* dose. Shit. Every time I ship out. Private doctor. King-size shot of penicillin. Streptomycin. Sulfa. Those dirty whores with their rotting cunts. Eighteen months of needles. Still. After a couple of days. Wake up with a tear every morning. And Jesus. Now that stupid doll. If I don't take my turn, those bastards will all give me the raspberries. But if I *do* screw the stupid thing, they'll *all* end up with gonorrhea.

The Deacon hung his head over the coffee cup, the muscles in his cheeks knotting and relaxing.

Chaude pisse. That's what those Canuck lumberjacks call it back home. Hot piss. And they're not kidding. Every time I go to the head. East Africa. Them Durban broads. The American girls they call 'em. And Reggie. Spent every dime he could draw. Must have screwed seven of 'em. Different one every night. Even two a night. He was probably the one who passed the clap around. Then got himself cured on the side. And said nothin'. Crazy bastard. Probably picked it up in one of them grass huts outside Dar es Salaam. He'd screw them filthy natives alright. Reggie? He'd fuck a zebra. A *boy* zebra. He'd spend his last dollar to buy a ladder to fuck a giraffe with.

The Deacon picked up his cup and put it in the sink in the pantry, dropping his cigarette butt into the garbage can. The focsle was quiet as he went in. All the lights were out except his own reading lamp shining from the bulkhead like a small spotlight, revealing the doll in the middle of the room hanging upside down, her left ankle suspended from the handle of the mushroom ventilator in the overhead. Swinging back and forth with the motion of the ship, Cynthia turned around in a slow spin as her hands dragged on the deck, her hair hanging down, her right leg flopping forward, her breasts sagging.

Reggie tried to muffle his giggle with a pillow.

Boy. What a pair of clowns I got for watch partners.

Go to bed, willya? And turn off that fuckin' light. The rotten bitch is only gettin' what she deserves.

But what's the idea, Whitey?

You said you didn't want her. Right? But we thought

we'd let her hang around anyway. Let her twat cool off a while.

But what kind of a thing is that to have hangin' right there in the middle of the room? It's creepy.

Go to bed. Read your Bible. Say your prayers or somethin'.

The Deacon clambered up on his bunk, covered himself and put out the light. He rolled over. But he could still hear the soft drag and rub of Cynthia's hands as she swung back and forth in the darkness, scratching helplessly at the deck.

● SANITARY SAM went into the Deck Department head and scrubbed out the toilet bowls with a brush. He did the sinks and polished the mirrors. With a little Comet on a rag, he soogeed away the hand marks he found on the bulkheads. Then he filled a bucket with water and began to swab the passageway, pausing to dunk the mop and wring it out. He started in front of the Bosun's room and worked his way aft until he reached the twelve-to-four focsle at the very edge of Engine Department territory.

He crept inside and began picking up the shoes to put them on the bench out of his way. But when he straightened up he flinched, startled by the doll. Sanitary Sam looked at each of the three men. Satisfied that the snores were genuine, he pushed the mop back and forth. There was a creak somewhere inside the bulkhead. The ship rolled. The doll slowly swung toward him, her fingers dragging across the worn red deck. Quivering, he looked at the sleeping men again and then carefully squeezed past the doll to mop the corner, leaving a dry spot in the middle of the room where Cynthia's hands were restlessly groping. When Cynthia's head bumped up against his leg, he gasped, his mouth open and tremulous. He turned to resume his work but his elbow hit her stomach. As he glanced at her pubic hair, the doll gave a lurch. Sam stiffened. He made a few quick moves with the mop, looked at the men of the twelve-to-four, then stretched up on tiptoe, his eyebrows raised and his lips pouted as he stared into the hole exposed by the one dangling leg.

Sam went outside. He cleaned the other focsles as

quickly as he could. Putting away his bucket and swab, his cleanser and rags, he sneaked back into the twelve-to-four, his mouth open and very dry. Holding the doll around the waist, her free leg over his shoulder, Sam reached up and untied the half hitches. Her left leg suddenly fell, flopping over his other shoulder, her buttocks turned up in his face. He waddled to the door, Cynthia's limbs quivering and elastic as he wrestled her out to the passageway and then into his own room. Dropping her on Phillips' single lower bunk, Sam locked the door. Clapping his hands together with a quick, fluttering applause, his feet did a prancing jig.

His fingers shaking, Sam straightened the doll, arranging her hair, patting her on both cheeks, gingerly pinching her nipples. He opened his locker and reached inside for the packages that he had been saving for Manila, the panties and the brassieres, the nylons and cosmetics that he always bought before he shipped out, knowing this would give him an edge on any waterfront in the world. Sam broke the strings and tore open the paper wrappings. Putting a cellophane envelope between his teeth, he jerked it open, taking out a pair of thirty-denier nylons, holding them up to the light in the porthole. Closing his eyes, he let the fragile, sheer material brush over his face.

Rolling the stockings down, he drew them over Cynthia's feet and legs, pulling them snug and smoothing the wrinkles. He took out a pair of black lace panties from one of the thin cardboard boxes and chose a black brassiere from the various sizes and colors he had in the bag. But he stopped. Taking a bath towel, he hung it in front of the open porthole, securing it between the glass and the steel cover held up by a short chain.

He pulled the panties over Cynthia's hips and buttocks. Inserting her arms through the brassiere straps, he pushed her breasts into the cups and rolled her over on her side to fasten the hooks. Sam grinned down at Cynthia.

But his expression changed. His lips pouted and tears formed in his eyes. With a whimper and a tight sob, he fell on top of her, chewing desperately on her brassiere.

Psss*st*. Hey. Hey, *Sam*.

Catching his breath with a sharp choke, Sanitary Sam looked over his shoulder. He got up and crossed the focsle, pulling the towel a few inches away from the porthole to look out into the anxious, shining black face of the Crew Messman.

Sam. Listen. You got the doll? Right? Ah mean. It's your turn now, ain't it? Ah heard them othuh rope chokers talkin' 'bout each watch takin' turns. Right? Say, man. How 'bout lettin' me have a crack at that doll baby? Okay?

Uh uh, Zeke. This is only for the Deck Department.

Oh, man. Fuck that shit. Damn the gawd-dam' Deck Department. Whut ah wont to do is make you a deal, man. Look here. It's your turn. Right? Ah mean. You kin do whut you wont to. Right? Fuck her. Suck her. Beat her with a stick. Right? So how 'bout rentin' her out? Jes for a few minutes. Man, it don' take me long. Bam-bam. Thank you, ma'am. That's me.

No. I can't. The fellas would get mad.

Like that motheroo Phillips, you mean? Nevah mind that Mistuh Charley bastard. Fuck 'im. Look man. Whut ah'll do is. Ah got a box of Hershey bars here. Ah bought 'em the last time the Ole Man opened up the Slop Chest. Ah mean. Whut good is money way out here? Right? But whut *ah* got is real *eat*in'.

Sanitary Sam was silent.

A whole box ah'm talkin' 'bout. Not no half box.

Sanitary Sam licked his lips, then drew in his lower lip with his teeth and bit down on it.

All you gotta do is let me come in the room. Punchy is out on deck foolin' aroun' with his jump rope. Phillips is on the wheel. Right? Look. Ah got me a coffee pot full o' hot water. Right here. Come on. Take the screen out'n this porthole so you can see these here Hershey bars.

Zeke pushed in the round screen which fell on the bench. Grinning, he held up the percolator and the candy.

Ah'm comin' 'round, Sam. Okay? You unlock that there door and let me in. Tha's all you gotta do. Right?

Zeke turned away. In a moment there was a light knock on the focsle door. Chewing his lip, Sam reached toward the key, then pulled his hand back, his fingers trembling. There was another knock. Sam turned the key but jerked his hand away, not touching the knob. The door opened. Zeke slipped inside. With a big grin, he presented Sam with the candy.

Here you are, mah boy. Now. Where is she? Oh, yeah. *There* she is. All blond and pink and juicy. Hey, man. Tha's crazy. You got her all dressed up. Where'd you git all this stuff? Damn. Oh, damn, she looks real. She looks jes like a ofay lady ah used to know back home. Used to run a general store a mile and a half up the road. Mah momma did all our tradin' there. She had hair jes like this gal does. Oh, man. Look at that brassiere and them panties. Hot *damn*. Look, Sam. Why don't you go on out a few minutes? Swab the deck in the head again. Or go to work on the toilet bowls some more.

Sanitary Sam left the focsle, taking two Hershey bars, his lips smacking loudly as he crunched the almonds with his teeth and sucked on the chocolate.

Since it was Sunday the deck gang did no work except to stand the wheel watches and do the sanitary work. Punchy was exercising on the fantail with the bag, his feet apart and braced against the pitch and roll of the ship, swinging forehand and backhand, left and right, pounding away without pause. At nine-thirty he went inside to the pantry where he filled the percolators and plugged them in for coffee time.

When Phillips was relieved, he went below to his room. Sam was sitting on the bench, eating a Hershey bar, his lips smacking loudly. Cynthia lay naked on Phillips' bunk.

Hot damn, Sam. You're right on the ball. You grabbed our sweet li'l baby doll early. Nevah min' waitin' till we call the watch. And she's rarin' to go, too. Hell, she's even warm. How 'bout that? You're whut ah calls a *real* watch partner. Now. How 'bout bein' a sport and lettin' me have jes a li'l privacy? Ah jes wont to tear off a quick hunk. 'Stead o' coffee time. Ah'll have me a li'l nooky time.

Sam reached into his locker for a Hershey bar and went out. Phillips locked the door. He gloated over the beauty of the doll, fondling her breasts with both hands until his eyes fell on the photographs of his wife and his two children that were Scotch-taped to the bulkhead over his bunk. Between the pictures was fastened a miniature Confederate flag. With a scowl, he took the pictures down and put them in his locker before kicking off his shoes and lying down next to Cynthia.

● IN THE AFTERNOON the sky was heavily overcast, the wind increasing until the swells were streaked with foam from the breaking crests. Stamas, the four-to-eight Fireman, climbed the jury ladder and the catwalk, strolling over the deck cargo, the wind rumpling his hair and tearing the ash off his cigarette. He leaned casually on the two-by-four railing as though he were on a boardwalk at some beach resort. Then he tried the handle of the door of one of the automobiles, opened it, climbed in and sat in the driver's seat. He smoked his cigarette. Gently he laid his hand on the bottom arc of the steering wheel. With small movements he jiggled the wheel back and forth, staring through the brine-colored windshield and over the stern of the ship, watching the bubbling wake that boiled away in a wide, turbulent path of foam straight back to the horizon.

After lunch the Bosun went out on deck to take a look at the ship's gear. Just aft of number five hatch were some drums that had been taken aboard in New York, fish oil, Consol oil and hull paint, all roped against each other behind the hatch coaming by an intricate series of loops, round turns and rolling hitches. But the sailors had used new line, which had since stretched under the strain of the shifting weights and the alternate wetting and drying of the weather. The Bosun went forward to his focsle to break out the Carpenter to help him resecure the drums. But Chips grumbled and complained.

What are you bitchin' about, Chips? It's overtime.

Overtime, shit. I wanna lay in my sack. It's Sunday.

But I need you out here. I gotta have a set of fingers.

Alright. Damn it. Alright. But we wouldn't have this kind of weather if those young punks would pay their whores.

Come on. Everybody paid. It's just Cape Hatteras is all.

Hatteras, my ass. I'm tellin' you. This is a *jinx* wind. It's that damn doll. I'd rather whistle up a storm in the wheelhouse for a whole week than have a woman on the ship.

But Cynthia ain't no woman. She's only a doll.

Yeah? Some doll. Ever since she came aboard. The weather went to hell right away. What I want to know is. What's she for? Where'd she come from? Huh? What does she *want?*

Come on, Chips. You make her out like she was human.

She's an image, ain't she? Huh? A female image? Like the one who came aboard my ship in Baltimore? Visitors, they said. Oh, yeah. Sure. Made goo-goo eyes at me until I had a hard-on so bad I jumped ship. *Deserted,* by God. Then she turned out to be nothin' but a tease. You think that wasn't a put-up job?

Chips. *Chips.* You told me that story *before.* It happened in nineteen *ten.* When you were in sail. You were a cadet. A kid on a school ship. So you jumped ship. So what?

So *what?* I could have been an officer. In the Imperial Navy. I could have had a command. Flag rank, maybe. *That's* what.

In the *Ger*man navy? You're nuts. Been two wars since then. Haven't had a king over there for forty fuckin' years. Or ain't you heard? Hell. You been American practically all your life.

Damn jinx. Suck the juice right out of your bones

until a man's a dry stick. Wood. That's what we got these days. Iron ships and wooden men.

Look. You want me to *pay* Cynthia? Would that make you feel better? I'll open up a bank account in her name. How's that?

Throw her over the side. *Then* I'll feel better. Let her wiggle her god-damn ass on some other ship.

Come on, Chips. That's a regular goddess of love we got. Everybody's gotta have a Venus for the penis.

Ha, ha. You won't laugh so hard if this garbage barge cracks up on a reef. Or busts in two pieces.

Listen. All I asked was. Come on out on deck and give me a hand. Get yourself some gravy overtime. Twenty minutes' work for a two-hour minimum. Huh? So what do I get? A lot of superstitious bullshit. Listen. We ain't got sails no more. Right? You ain't a kid no more. Right? You ain't a German no more and accordin' to you. You can't even get a hard-on no more. Right? So forget it. It's all over. Okay?

That night the ship began to pitch very heavily. The low-pressure area had passed to the north, the circular pattern of the wind backing until it came from astern, the swell lifting the propeller out of the water, the engine racing, the hull shaking. Each time the bow pounded, it sent up a cloud of spray, Charley Phillips ducking below the apron, hugging himself in his black rubber slicker and tasting the salt on his face as he was tossed thirty feet upward and then suddenly dropped. Down below in the chain locker there was a loud clatter and a clang as a link of the anchor cable fell off the heaped pyramid. And again the bow pounded, shuddering, the plates in the hull creaking and squealing with gradually decreasing spasms. Phillips snatched open the telephone box, turning the handle violently. He pressed the button on the receiver and waited.

Bridge?

Hey, Mate. Christ Almighty. Ah cain't stay up here no more. The gawd-dam' seas are comin' over the bulwarks. Whut you tryin' to do? Git me washed over the fuckin' side?

Hey, wait a minute. Take it easy.

Take it *easy?*

Yeah. Take it easy. I'm the officer in charge of this watch, god-damn it. And don't you forget it. If the seas are comin' over the bow, you should have told me.

Well. That's whut ah'm a-*do*in'. Ah'm *tell*in' yuh.

Okay. Then come on up to the flying bridge. And don't forget to tell the standby that you're moving the lookout.

Aw right. Aw right. Yes, *suh.* Ah'll jes *do* that.

Cursing the asshole officers who complicated his life, Phillips slammed the telephone box closed. As he started to walk aft, the ship began another series of pitches, the bow slamming harder and harder, sending up exploded clouds of spray shining high up in the glare from the masthead light. The bow dropped suddenly and he became almost weightless, his feet barely touching the surface of the deck. There was a tremendous boom, water pouring through the mooring chocks and sloshing over Phillips' sea boots. He stiffened his legs, his knees bending under the upward thrust of thousands of tons as the bow rose high up in the air.

Nobody wanted to play pinochle and the messhall was deserted. Chips went to bed early, jamming his life preserver between the edge of the mattress and the side rail to keep his body from rolling from side to side. But he was unable to sleep, listening to the wheelhouse bell tolling away the half-hours, staring up at the overhead, feeling the mattress curving around his back and shoulders and remembering the hug and the swing of his hammock when he was on the brigantine *Kaiser Wilhelm* and his rating was Seekadett and he was fifteen years old.

The bow pounded again. He could hear the water sloshing over the deck outside and splashing overboard through the scuppers. He could hear distant thunder and lightning. The Bosun was snoring on the other side of the room, lying next to the nude doll whose smooth white skin was glowing in the darkness, as obscure, as lovely and as evil as any succubus ghost. The Carpenter listened to the wind and the tortured sounds of the ship. Up in the wheel-house two bells were sounded.

Bitch. Tease a man to his ruin. Torture him with your eyes and your ass. Then laugh at him. Turn him into a bum. Career. Family. Personal honor. Alles. Alles aber auch alles ist zum Teufel. Wegen *dir*. Verdammte Hur'.

There was a loud crack of lightning. Chips sat up in his bunk, straining to peer out the porthole, his eyes bulging, his wrinkled old face cruel and haunted.

He got up and carefully crept across the focsle to the Bosun's bunk, looking down at the doll. Very slowly he picked her up, easing her away. Quietly he opened the door and carried her out into the passageway, barefooted and wearing only his shorts. He opened the dogs that clamped the storm door shut, forcing it back and dragging the doll outside. Water washed over his feet, one hand holding the grab rail along the side of the house as he fought against the force of the wind and the heavy downpour of rain. When he reached number four hatch, he stretched her out on her back and looked up at the sky.

Alright. Now drain the juice out of that storm up there. Let old man Neptune get a piece of your ass. Here. Gott verdammte Hex'. Und du hast mir schon alles versaut.

Chips went over to the schooner guy, the wet, heavy bundle of manila swaying with every roll of the ship, hanging under the boom and just clearing the hatch. He untied the clove hitches and pulled off several fathoms of rope. He held it up in both hands, straddling the doll's body as he hissed and growled with a malevolent snarl.

See? Like this. Open up wide. Make a circle. Swallow up the lightning. And the wind. The whole sky. The ocean. Die ganze Welt. And then slowly make a hitch. An overhand knot. And then—draw it up—*tight*—

There was a bright, crackling flash of lightning that illuminated the booms, the mast, the hatch and the old Carpenter who cavorted in his dripping shorts, waving a bight of knotted line around his head, the doll lying at his feet, her legs spread wide, her eyes closed, her smile peaceful.

● ON MONDAY the Captain opened the Slop Chest, a line of men standing in the passageway, waiting their turn to buy candy, cigarettes, hair tonic, work clothes, gloves and shoes, each man signing for his slops in the notebook.

On Tuesday the Captain held a sanitary inspection, making the rounds of the ship with the Chief Mate, the Chief Engineer and the Chief Steward. He went through the galley, the messhalls and the pantry. He inspected the storerooms and the chill boxes. He looked at the decks and the bulkheads in the passageways, in the heads and in the showers. And then he went into some of the crew focsles, including the room shared by the Pantryman, the Saloon Messman and the Bedroom Steward.

Whiskey Bill lay on his back in a pair of red polka-dot shorts. He was snoring, his pink, hairy, mountainous belly slowly rising and falling. His upper teeth were capped with a set of plastic Dracula vampire fangs which protruded from his mouth. Extending three inches out of his eyesockets was a pair of corkscrew-shaped, red-veined, popping zombie eyes which stared at the Captain with an evil, watchful, all-knowing glare. Whiskey Bill continued to snore as the Captain stooped over him, sniffing.

This man's been *drinking*. He has *liquor* on board.

The Captain saw a half-filled glass on the deck next to Harrison's shoes. Snatching it up, he showed it to his chief officers with an expression of triumph and outrage which quickly turned to bewilderment when he realized the fluid simply would not pour. The "liquor" was really a solid core of amber-colored glass.

Captain Pedersen let out a roar.

This man is *drunk!* I want the room *searched! NOW!*

Whiskey Bill sat up with a jerk, the Captain shaking the dummy shot glass in his fist.

Get up, you. I'm searching this room. You've got *booze* on board this ship. And I intend to find it.

Whiskey Bill grunted and moaned as he heaved himself out of the lower bunk, swaying, peering through the small holes in the pupils of the false eyes.

Open up your locker. Right now!

Snuffling his nose and dragging his bare feet, Whiskey Bill staggered to the corner of the small, cramped room, lumbering like a great, demented Balinese deity. The Chief Engineer drew away. The Chief Mate tried very hard not to grin. Swearing, Captain Pedersen shoved the Steward out of his way and shouldered Whiskey Bill aside, banging the metal locker door open and quickly running his hand through the various shelves. He whirled around.

Ha! So you've got it stashed. Huh?

The Captain pounced on Whiskey Bill's bunk, jerking away the pillow, the sheets, the folded blanket and lifting the mattress up around the edges. Then he stooped down and peered underneath, dragging out the steamer trunk. He tried the hasps and found them locked. Smiling, he looked up.

Okay. This is it. Where's the god-damn key?

Whiskey Bill's voice was muffled, his lips impaired by the protruding fangs.

Cap'n. I ain't got no booze on board. Honest.

*Bull*shit. Gimme that god-damn key. *Now!* That's a direct fucking order. As Master of this vessel, I am hereby conducting a legal, official search for contraband. I *order* you to give me that key.

Whiskey Bill fumbled in his locker and reluctantly handed over a key. The Captain unlocked the trunk and threw open the lid, staring down at the four cardboard whiskey cases.

No booze, you said. Huh? No *booze*?

Whiskey Bill slumped on the bench, his arms crossed, his belly and the red polka-dot shorts sagging down between his legs. The zombie eyes glared as the Captain opened the top of one of the cartons, peering into the empty compartments sectioned off by the cardboard partitions. He opened another carton. And then the third. He glanced up at Whiskey Bill. With a muttered curse, he dipped his hand into one of the compartments and pulled out an apple. Again his hand plunged down and came up with a pair of dirty socks. Very quickly, again and again he fumbled among the four cartons, snatching out a bag of salted peanuts, a banana, a pair of undershorts with a silkscreen painting of a robin pulling a worm out of the fly, a rubber scorpion, and finally an imitation shrunken head dangling from the Captain's fingers by its own hair.

A series of short muffled blasts of air snorted from Whiskey Bill's nose, his belly quivering with a profound, secret spasm, his smile suppressed behind the fangs, the fantastic eyes glaring as the Captain squatted on the deck, his face drained and contorted as he stared at the smooth, shiny, plastic dog turd that rested in the palm of his hand.

● JUST BEFORE SUPPER the Deck Engineer chalked a notice over the menu on the blackboard that there would be a union meeting at seven o'clock. During the meal there were a few grumbles, but Watkins insisted it was time to get things squared away, elect department delegates and prepare to settle any beefs that might arise during the trip. The crew began to collect in the messhall, most of them solemn and contrite, freshly shaven, their voices muted. Whitey sat in a corner. The Second Cook stared at a bulkhead, his lips moving, his hands twitching. Whiskey Bill sat hunched over a cup of coffee. Stamas held an open book in his lap. Cooper smoked his pipe, one elbow on the edge of the table, shielding his eyes with the palm of his hand. The last arrivals gathered in the pantry and in the passageway, peering through the doors, the overcrowded messhall already filled with smoke. Watkins drummed his fingers on the table and glanced repeatedly at the clock. Then he rapped his coffee cup on the table.

Okay. Let's come to order. First thing is to elect a chairman. Who's got some nominations?

Nobody spoke. The curious glanced around the room. Those who thought they might be conscripted were looking sheepishly away. The Second Cook muttered to his cigarette ash.

Give him a shotgun. Elect him by accla-MA-tion. I make a motion. I got the time. What the hell? Let's all get together and take the wrinkles out of the sheet.

Collins, the eight-to-twelve Oiler, spoke up:
What about you, Whitey?

Whitey snarled.

I decline. You take it. You're the legal eagle.

Several voices mumbled but the Second Cook's was louder:

Fuck 'im. Accla-MA-tion. That's what it's all about.

Watkins grinned around the room.

I have a motion made and seconded that Collins be elected by acclamation. All in favor?

There was a general grumble, a few distinct "ayes."

All opposed? The ayes have it and so ordered.

Collins changed seats with Watkins, his face stern.

Let's have a recording secretary. Any volunteers?

There was another silence. Sanitary Sam fidgeted, his voice squeaking as he blurted out:

The Bosun. I nominate the Bosun.

Everyone remained motionless. There wasn't a sound. After a pause of instinctive embarrassment, the Bosun jerked his hands out of his lap under the table, defiantly cupping them under his chin in plain sight. Without waiting for the rigamarole of a vote, the Bosun growled.

Aw right. Fuck it. I'll take the job.

Collins feebly tried to explain:

Never mind, Bos. Somebody'll take it. We can—

What's the matter? Don't think I can do it?

The Bosun held the pencil between his surviving little finger and the next nub. He wrote the date at the top of the minutes of the meeting, his hand moving stiffly as he shaped the words. Tilting his head, he watched the progress of the pencil point, then suddenly glared at the curious faces. Only Whitey continued to smirk without averting his eyes.

The Bosun looked away, frowned and puffed on his cigarette. He had been furious at Whitey ever since he woke up that morning and found Cynthia missing from his bunk, discovering her later sprawled out on number four hatch, abandoned, filthy and wet. But the Bosun had decided to bide his time and not say anything. The thieving bastard. Creeping into his room like some kind of a pervert rape artist.

Collins hit the cup on the table.

Let's have a minute of silence for our departed brothers.

Everyone stood up, the swivel chairs turning with the roll of the ship, hitting legs and banging against the edges of the tables. With their caps and their smokes in their hands, the men lowered their heads. Reggie caught Sanitary Sam's eye and repressed a giggle. Men scratched, coughed, flicked cigarette ashes into the sardine cans used for ashtrays. Collins rapped the cup on the table. Everyone sat down.

Under the order of "old business" it was brought up that nothing had been done about the repair list from the previous trip. It was decided to bring the matter up with the Chief Engineer and the Chief Mate. Under "new business" the various delegates were nominated and elected. Watkins became Ship's Delegate. The Deck Department elected Cooper. Collins was the Engine Department choice and Zeke was picked by the Steward's Department.

Collins exercised his chairmanship, using Robert's Rules to proceed from one order of business to the other, every step made into a motion, seconded and confirmed in a listless, mumbled affirmative. But then came "good and welfare." Whitey complained about the noise in the passageway while the twelve-to-four was trying to sleep. Men would hang their laundry on the handrails in the engineroom fidley and then would slam the steel door. But one of the firemen said wet clothes shouldn't be hanging in the fidley, anyway. They dripped down the ladders and the platforms into the fireroom below. The washing machine wasn't working properly. Watkins said nobody ever turned the motor off when he was finished. As Deck Engineer, it was his job to fix it but he couldn't repair burned-out pumps and bearings forever. There was discussion about installing an automatic timer on the switch but several men openly scoffed at getting anything as luxurious as that on the *Ocean Endeavor*.

And then the subject of food came up. The first tentative complaints quickly became an uproar. The night lunch was insufficient. There was too much rice on the menu. The meat was tough and overcooked. Hao Hai Ren, the Chinese Chief Cook, began to splutter his protests. The Chief Steward cowered, whining about the stores he had ordered but didn't get delivered, explaining how the Port Steward cut down on every stores list that was sent in. Zeke counterattacked. The watch standers were still leaving cups out and generally making a pigsty out of the messhall instead of putting things in the sink. It was not his job to clean up the messhall every morning before setting up for breakfast.

Chips changed the subject. The bell from the wheelhouse disturbed his sleep. The assembly politely heard out the oldtimer's beef. But the matter was left dangling, unresolved, unaccepted, yet not really denied. Everything was quiet. The Bosun caught up with his minutes, scribbling painfully. There was a nervous lull.

And then Zeke burst out angrily:

Whut about all the gawd-dam' discrimin-ation on this here ship? Huh? Ah keeps hearin' "niggah" all the gawd-dam' time.

Nobody said anything. There were averted looks.

What's your beef, Zeke? Nobody else been bitchin' about discrimination. You ain't the only colored guy on here.

Hell no, ah ain't. Same thing goes for them othuh Steward's Department guys. Ain't that right, now? Hey! Speak *up*, you guys. Come on there, Flip Flop. You Filipino fuckhead. *Say* somethin'. Chief? They always makin' fun o' you. Screwin' your name up. Callin' you How High

Can You Run. And Callin' you Hang Fang. Hey, Matan-zas? Don't they hard-time you for bein' Porto Rican?

The room was silent. The engine pounded and squealed. The bulkheads squeaked. The dishes rattled. Zeke looked desperate, searching the impassive faces. He swallowed, his fury hotter than ever.

Well. Damn it. Whut about that there doll, then? Huh? What about *that*? That ain't fuckin' discrimin-ation? So whut about it? All you Rope-Choker Department guys?

Collins rapped his coffee cup on the table.

You're out of order, Zeke. This is a personal matter.

Yeah. Damn right, it's personal.

The chair will entertain a motion to adjourn.

I make the motion.

I second it.

Motion made and seconded. All in favor.

Aye.

All opposed? Ayes have it. Meeting adjourned.

Collins rapped the coffee cup on the table. Everyone began to leave, Zeke pushing his way out to storm down the passageway to his room.

● ON MONDAY MORNING they saw Panama, the light on Punta Manzanillo breaking the horizon after the loom had been visible against the sky for half an hour. The Captain was in the chart room mumbling bitterly as the Second Mate plotted the bearing and the distance off.

Damn. Can't even maintain an eight-knot average. We're gonna end up bein' four hours late from New York.

Well. That isn't so bad. We had delays. We lowered the boat. We had some pretty bad weather. Can't blame you.

Bullshit. *Every*body blames me. That's what sailin' as Master is all about.

A convoy had just come out of Limon Bay and the traffic was heavy. In another two hours they could see the lights of Colón, Toro Point flashing distinctively from all the rest. The Chief Mate relieved the Second at four, the Captain still on the bridge, looking through his binoculars. At exactly 0436 the Chief Mate jingled the telegraph to signal Arrival. The engine room answered. The *Ocean Endeavor* entered through the breakwater, Captain Pedersen conning the vessel over to the anchorage.

Chips had already removed the devil claws. He took the windlass out of gear and stood by the brake handle. Captain Pedersen stopped the ship. After drifting for several minutes, he ordered hard left rudder. Standing out on the wing, he faced forward, cupped his hands around his mouth and bellowed out in a sing-song roar:

LET GO—THE STAR-BOARD AN-CHOR!!

Chips banged the iron bar against the brake handle. And then there was a clattering, exploding roar and a splash as the cable ran over the wildcat, clanking down the hawse pipe and into the water with a great cloud of rust and dried mud. The four-to-eight watch lowered the gangway and rigged cluster lights over the side. A launch came alongside. The quarantine officer came aboard and behind him the ship's agent, a canal official, the Pilot and an Apprentice Pilot.

At seven o'clock word was passed to commence heaving on the anchor. Britt was on the wheel, Cooper manning the water hose on the focsle head, washing the mud off the cable links as they came slowly clinking up the hawse pipe, the windlass groaning. When the anchor was clear of the water, Chips rang the ship's bell very rapidly.

The *Ocean Endeavor* sailed past the other ships in the anchorage, taking her place in the southbound convoy that moved down the channel toward Gatun Locks. While underway, a launch came alongside to put aboard a gang of Panamanian line handlers. The Pilot maneuvered the ship into the first of the three locks. Heaving lines were thrown ashore. Several sailors manned the winches as the line handlers hauled in the wire towing hawsers and made them fast. Three electric mules on each side moved slowly ahead, taking the *Endeavor* completely in tow, her engine stopped. The Pilot signaled to the mules with his whistle until the ship was dragged into position. The gate closed behind her stern and the water level immediately began to rise.

Britt relaxed when the pilot stepped into the wheelhouse and lit a cigarette. He watched the dripping wall of the lock chamber as the ship moved up its face. Agitated, he started to speak several times but stopped himself. Finally he blurted,

Mister Pilot? Sir? Please, sir. How much does it cost

for a ship to go through the canal? I got a good reason for askin'. I'm not just bein' curious.

Huh? Oh. It's ninety cents, I think. Per net ton.

Ninety cents. Uh, huh. So for a Liberty, it's what?

In round numbers, about four thousand dollars, I would imagine. But I don't handle the money. I only work here.

And so how much is the Suez Canal?

Su*ez*? I really couldn't say.

It'd be cheaper, wouldn't it? No locks to worry about? Well—maybe.

Captain Pedersen scowled. Britt scratched and fidgeted.

The bridge rose up past the wall of concrete covered with slime and moss. And then they could look out over the neat lawns and the white buildings of the Canal Zone, the jungle and the green hills in the distance. The forward gate swung open and the mules began to haul the ship ahead, growling and clattering up the forty-five-degree incline of the walls. The crew lined the bulwarks. The officers leaned on the railings of the boat deck. They smoked. They talked. They stared at the mules and the drivers, looked at the tower with the cones and balls hoisted on halyards to signal the pilots of the convoy. And they wondered about those narrow roads which led off to the green forests they could see in the distance.

And then again, into the third lock. As they escalated upward, other ships were following behind them. On the other side of the double locks, ships in the northbound convoy were climbing down. When the upper gate swung open the mules slacked off their towing wires. The line handlers threw the spliced eyes off the bitts. The Pilot ordered slow ahead and the *Endeavor* moved out of the lock into Gatun Lake.

Mister Teier studied the chart of the canal in order

to identify the reaches, cuts and channels that zigzagged across the isthmus. He put the names and the times in the log book and then looked out over the water and the jungle, the ship sailing along the old courses of submerged river valleys, around green hills and over mountain divides. The water was perfectly calm, the bow wave a shining curl as the ship slid over the surface with a faint, muffled throb. Mister Teier went outside to read the thermometer for his log-book entries. It was ninety-six degrees. He described the weather as "partly cloudy, intermittent brief showers."

When Captain Pedersen came in and sat down at the table reserved for him and the Chief Engineer, the Saloon Messman handed him the menu, knowing he would merely glance at it and order the usual thing.

I'll have a full house on the vegetables.

Yes, sir. Foll 'ouse on vege-table.

Better watch that meat, Chief. That cholesterol's gonna clog up your pipes one of these days.

Mister McKnight grunted.

The clock on the bulkhead began to chime eight bells. The engine room telegraph was rung and answered for the noon test. The whistle blasted. The general alarm was sounded with a brief touch. Matanzas went down the passageway to the galley, where the Second Cook dished up every vegetable on the menu, carefully wiping off the edge of the plate with his apron, knowing that the order was for the Old Man.

When the Captain finished his meal, he went up to the bridge deck. As he passed the radio shack he saw Sparks with his feet propped up on the control panel, scribbling a routine weather report on the margin of a *Playboy* magazine as the radio stuttered out its coded static. Inside his office, the Captain unlocked a desk drawer and took out a bottle and a shot glass, pouring himself a drink, which he downed with one swallow. He replaced the bottle, took a cigar out of the box and locked the drawer. He went out on the small deck that hung like a balcony at the rear of the house. Putting one foot on the lowest guardrail, he leaned both elbows on top. As he exhaled the smoke he took the cigar out of his mouth and twisted it in his fingers, looking out over the engine-room skylight, number four hatch, the deckload of olive-drab cargo containers and the four privately owned vehicles, which to the Army people were P.O.V.'s.

The *Endeavor* was passing close to the island of Barro Colorado, a piece of virgin Panamanian jungle kept intact as a game preserve. A light shower began and just as suddenly it stopped. The Captain considered the Wisconsin license plate on the rear of the Chevrolet Impala on the starboard side. And he considered Giorgio Stamas, the four-to-eight Fireman, who sat in the driver's seat, one arm resting on the open windowsill, one hand lightly on the steering wheel.

Captain Pedersen grumbled to himself:

Stupid bastard. Does he really think he's drivin' down some turnpike goin' backwards? Fuckin' car nut. He ought to get a job in a parkin' lot instead of goin' to sea.

The Captain took another drag on his cigar and changed feet on the guardrail. He hated deck cargoes. But then they had to go and put four automobiles on *top*. How the hell could the sailors possibly raise and lower the booms at number five hatch without scratching the shit out of the body paint with the preventers and the guy pennants?

Then the Captain saw Punchy coming out of the house with Cynthia slung under his arm. Punchy shuffled in heavy, unlaced work shoes over to number four hatch. He dropped the doll on her back, her legs dangling over the edge of the coaming, her face turned upward with a dreamy expression. Punchy disappeared. In a moment he was back with a three-quarter-inch water hose used by the deck gang for soogeeing the house. He pulled over some slack, twisted the nozzle and began hosing her down.

Captain Pedersen stood up straight, frowning as he jammed the cigar into his mouth, thrusting it upward at an angle.

Punchy scrubbed the doll with a stiff laundry brush and a bar of yellow soap. When she was completely covered with lather, he turned on the hose and sprayed her again, lifting one leg by the ankle and inserting the nozzle into her vagina. The water gushed out over the tarpaulin, the hatch coaming and the wedges and cleats, running down over the deck to form a puddle under his shoes. He turned off the nozzle. He unscrewed Cynthia's navel and rolled her over, dragging her off the hatch to hold her around the middle. The water splashed out on the deck as Cynthia squatted with bent knees.

Captain Pedersen paced back and forth but then returned to his place at the rail. He took several quick puffs on his cigar, watching Punchy as he tossed Cynthia back up on the hatch. He replaced her navel, turned her over and began to scrub her back, her buttocks and legs. Once more he gave her a rinse and then another thorough douching. He turned off the hose and coiled it neatly beside the potable-water manifold. Very briskly he dried Cynthia off with a towel, slung her over his shoulder and disappeared.

Captain Pedersen squinted at the cigar, threw it over the side and went back to his room, slamming the screen door.

The *Ocean Endeavor* reached the end of Gatun Lake and entered Gaillard Cut, an enormous ditch that went eight miles straight through the mountains. The channel narrowed and the opposing convoys passed very close, their engines stopped so the suction of the propellers would not draw their sterns together, the crews staring at the design, the equipment and the condition of each other's vessels.

Whiskey Bill was wearing a flaming orange and yellow aloha shirt. He sat on a mooring bitt, holding a coffee cup and watching the passing regatta. Cooper leaned on the bulwarks, a towel wrapped around his middle, his bare feet in a pair of Japanese zoris. Others lounged on the foredeck and on number three hatch to catch the breeze, some stretched out on cots in their underwear getting suntans, some reading, some listening to music from Panama City on a portable transistor radio.

So listen. I never finished tellin' you about that Italian broad.

Italian broad? Oh. *Her.* Yeah. Well. So what happened?

Well. What happened was. This was some Italian broad from Brooklyn who was married to some guy over in Jersey City. Every once in a while she'd come over for a visit. But like she'd tell the family she was in town for three days. Only thing is. She'd tell her husband she's gonna be gone for a week. She said that her family and her husband didn't get along too well. So it was easy to keep 'em from gettin' their heads together. Well. Right away I got the whole picture. This dame was strictly out for kicks. So the next thing I know, it's pretty near three in the morning and we're pretty friendly over there in that old booth. We're holdin' hands and we're playin' footsies and kneesies. But I didn't try to cop a real feel or anything 'cause there was a pretty good crowd in there.

Whiskey Bill paused and slowly sipped from the cup. Leaning forward, he placed it on top of the bulwark. Cooper glanced at Bill and then at the cup, reaching for it and taking a few small, rapid sips. He shut his eyes, swallowed and massaged his lips against each other, the movement distorting his face.

Well. It's about time for the joint to close. So I says
—How about comin' up to this room I got? It's only upstairs and I got a radio up there and I can get a bottle of
Scotch from the bartender. She hems and haws a little bit
and then she says okay. But she wants us to leave separate
so nobody'll suspect nothin'. You know how it is. So she
gets up and goes out. I waits five minutes and then I gets
up, too. I tells Tommy I'm gonna hit the sack. And I tells
him to stick a bottle of Johnny Walker Black Label in a
paper bag and slip it to me and put it down on my tab.
Tommy gives me another funny look. Beef Stew is still
sittin' there, too. But by this time he's knocked clear out
of his feeble, fuckin' mind. He's gigglin' so hard he damn
near fell off the stool. So I say to him—So long, Smitty. I
hope there ain't no hard feelin's about the *Peabody*. And
he says—Naw. That's okay, Whiskey. Bygones be bygones.
Then he starts gigglin' again. So I strolls out and I meets
this broad around the corner and we go through the side
door and then upstairs to my room. Oh, man. What a
night. I'm tellin' *you*. First I turns on the radio and I fixes
her a drink. Then I loves her up a little bit and then I
tosses her up on the sack. At first, after all that booze, I
only had about a semi hard-on. But after *that*. Boom. A
quick flick of the dick and I'm in like a burglar. She was
really ready for it too. She's got her legs up in the air and
she's moanin' and groanin' and scratchin' the hell out of
my back.

A ship called the *Del Mondo* was flying the Argentine
flag. A Finnish ship went by; the *Kusaa*. They met a Nor-
wegian whaler with four stacks and a huge hole in its
stern for hauling aboard its catch. There was a Dutchman,
a Swede and a Greek, a British tanker named the *Templar*
and then another American with an enormous deckload of
lumber piled up as high as the wheelhouse windows and
lashed down with monstrous chains and turnbuckles.

Whiskey Bill went on:

Anyway. We rested for a while and then had some more Johnny Walker. And the *next* thing you know, we're doin' the tango to this radio music, both of us bare-ass naked. And then—boom! Right back to el sacko. Anyhow. I finally passes out. I mean. You know. By that time my timber was pretty limber. So I didn't wake up until about three in the afternoon. I had about half a headache and wasn't feelin' any too good. But this New Jersey broad was still out cold. I tried to get a little action out of her. I was half hung over alright but I sure as hell wasn't *sen*ile. But I couldn't get this babe to even move. I slapped her a few times, but it was no use. So I decided to sneak downstairs to get myself an eye opener. Tommy had already opened up the joint. He works night and day, that guy. Seems like ever since he got married suddenly he's ambitious or somethin'. Anyhow. I says—Whaddaya say, Tommy? And he comes slidin' up real easy to where I'm sittin' and he whispers out of the corner of his mouth— Bill. Get the hell out of here. You got Togliatti trouble. So I says—What the hell's a Togliatti? And he says—It's a hole in the head if that tribe of baboons ever gets a hold of you. But no sense tellin' you anything. I spent twenty minutes last night givin' you the high sign. I did everything but send you a wire by Western Union. But can you take a hint? Oh, no. You're over there dancin' and prancin' and flyin' around. So this guy Tommy is a real worry wart, you know? And I'm not feelin' so good what with this headache and all. So I says—Tommy. Would you mind tellin' me what the hell you're talkin' about? And Tommy, he sticks his head up real close and he says—Whiskey. That broad you were tryin' to make out with is part of the Togliatti family. They're the toughest bunch of cutthroats in Brooklyn. They got the rackets in six different neighborhoods sewed up tight. They were in here this morning and they done got the word that you were the last one seen with Louise. She's the youngest sister of the Togliatti boys. Of which here ain't no less than six. And this sister is missin' and they're lookin' for her. And they figure they better find you first. If I was you, I'd leave town first. Then Tommy asks me, real quiet—Bill. You didn't shack up with her, did you? And I says—Hell, yes. Whaddaya think? She's upstairs right now. Passed out cold. Well. Tommy just about wet his pants.

Whiskey Bill chuckled, controlled himself and squinted one eye. He stretched his arm out for the coffee cup, staring down into it before taking another quick sip. Cooper lit his pipe and looked out over the side at the distant hills and jungle.

Several men motioned, a group forming at the bulwarks to watch a ninety-foot yacht go by, her sails furled and moving under auxiliary power alone, teak decks bleached, brightwork gleaming, the men in white shorts and Topsider shoes, the women in bathing suits. The crew of the *Endeavor* stared down in silence as the sleek image of luxury and importance quickly floated past.

Well. Tommy lets out this shriek. Upstairs? What's she doin' *upstairs?* Oh, Jesus. Oh, Mary Mother of God. Bill. Leave. Will you please *go?* This broad is married to Harry the Hustler. The boss of the Jersey City mobs. Get the hell outta *here! Now!* Anyhow. I got the picture alright. So I started to jump up and shag-ass upstairs. But then I looked at Tommy. I thought he had a case of the bends or somethin'. But then I sees this broad comin' through the door with six of the hairiest goons I ever did see. Well. All six of 'em gives me a real fishy look and then they sits in a front booth up by the door. But the dame, she comes marchin' up and plops herself down at the bar right next to me. And she says—Are you Whiskey Bill? And so I says—Yeah. That's what they call me. I don't know why, though. Hell. I'll drink anything. And I starts to chuckle. You know. I'm a free and easy, good-natured guy. And then I says—You wanna drink or anything?

Wow. I never seen a tougher-lookin' babe in my whole life. And about as ugly as a can full o' worms, too. But she just gives me this snarl and she says—Shut up, Buster. I'll buy my own god-damn drinks. And then she takes this cigarette out of her purse. She lights it up and then she lays her purse down on the bar without closin' it. And there inside, winkin' its eye at me, was this little pearl-handled pistol.

Kusasavitch came out on deck and began skipping rope. He jumped with different patterns; twice with each alternating foot, then with both feet at once as the rawhide leather whistled, the ball bearings whirring in the wooden handles. Punchy walked up and down, his chest heaving, the sweat dripping. He did another round of jumps, draped the skip rope around his neck and went back to the fantail to work out with his punching bag.

So when this Miss Dracula sees that I got a good peek at the pistol, she growls out—Aw right, *Mister* Son of a Bitch. Where the hell is she? And I says—Where's who? I was too god-damn nervous to think of anything else to say. As a matter of fact, what else *could* I say? But she comes right back with—You know damn well who. My kid sister, Louise. So right away I pulls a frown like I'm thinkin' real hard and I says—Lou*ise?* Oh. You must mean the young lady I was having a little chat with yesterday evening. Oh, man. I figured I'd better get with it and soft-soap this babe before she started to get violent or somethin'. But right away she comes back with—Cut out the bullshit. My sister didn't get home to her place in Jersey last night. Her old man's ready to start a gang war about it. She wasn't with us. But we *do* know she was seen in here last night with *you.* Well. When she said "we" I knew she was referrin' to that firin' squad sittin' over there in the booth. Like this one goon. All this time he's eatin' a bag of peanuts. He's tossin' 'em up to his mouth and he's chompin' away. But then he misses and a couple of these peanuts went down the neck of his shirt. You should have seen that moron. He's squirmin' and scratchin' and reachin' down inside his shirt for them nuts. Then, real easy, he takes out his shirt tail a little at a time, so they wouldn't fall out and land on the floor. The way he made such a production out of it you'd think them nuts were worth a dollar and a half a piece.

Approaching San Miguel, the ship maneuvered until the line handlers heaved aboard the wire hawsers from the mules. The ship was hauled into the lock chamber and the double gates closed. As the water was drained out of the chamber, a passenger ship from Australia was being lifted simultaneously in the opposite lock, the two vessels passing each other vertically, the passengers lining the rails.

Anyway. I'm still thinkin', see? So then I opens up with this real intriguin' smile and I says—Well, well. Louise didn't tell me about having such a charming family. She did say she was visiting relatives but she didn't elaborate. And I didn't want to pry into any personal—But Miss Dracula cut me off. Shut up, she says. And her teeth was bared like she was all ready to spring for my throat. So I says—Look. I met her here last night and we sat around havin' a few drinks until about three o'clock. I didn't even know she was married or had a family or she was supposed to be visitin' *any*body. I bought her a few drinks. We chewed the fat. And then she got up and left. I don't know *where* she went. It was none of my business and I didn't ask. Now there's nothin' wrong with that. Is there? But she snarls again. Real vicious.—Cut it. We *know* Louise. And we heard all about *you*, too. Where you live at? So I tells her—I'm stayin' at the Dog House. Oh, *Christ.* She makes a grab for her purse and she growls— Don't get funny, bastard. I'm fed up with your wisecracks already.

Whiskey Bill sipped from the coffee cup and passed it to Cooper. He took a small swallow and handed it back.

But I breaks in real quick—Wait a minute. The Dog House is what everybody calls the Seaman's Church Institute over on South Street in Manhattan. It's this great big monstrous flophouse especially reserved for nothin' but us merchant seamen. I *always* stay there when I'm in town. Well. That made her hesitate a second. And she says —Yeah? So what are you doin' over here in Brooklyn? So I explains. I says—Well. Me and Tommy here used to ship out together. That was before he decided to swallow the anchor and got married. Him and me been knowin' each other for years. But Tommy. Real nonchalant, he says— I've seen him around. He comes in once in a while for a couple of drinks. And he nods his head in my direction like I'm a god-damn stranger. I didn't dare say it. Not with Dragon Twat sittin' there. But I'm thinkin' to myself—I'll fix you. Bastard. Just wait 'til your wife finds out what *else* goes on in that room upstairs while I'm out at sea.

Whiskey Bill frowned and took a sip from the cup. He pursed his lips and looked over at the rising passenger ship.

Cooper saw an attractive, athletic young woman in a pleated white skirt standing by the rail of the promenade deck. He hesitated, glancing at Whiskey Bill and the others. Stiffly he moved his hand in a short wave. But without hesitation the woman smiled and waved back. Cooper's chest felt tight, his heartbeat increasing as he grinned across the gap of water and concrete, the woman slowly moving up as he sank down, one of them headed east, the other west.

Anyway. Right about then I couldn't think of nothin' to *say*. I mean. Nobody else was sayin' nothin', either. Tommy stood on one foot and then on the other foot. The boys in the booth and this Lena the Hyena dame, they just sat there and looked at *me*. For at least two or three hours. It was just like a movie projector had got stuck just when everybody was ready to make a fast draw. But right about then. This skinny, old, worn-out, fuckin' rum-dum walks through the door and comes shakin' his way up to the bar all hung over and bent out of shape. He sits there and looks around waitin' for somebody to serve him. But nobody moves. He blinks and nods and swallows a few times. And then he gets up and stumbles over to the jukebox. He drops in a quarter, punches a few buttons and sits back down. Everything's quiet. The jukebox is clickin' and hummin' and swallowin' this quarter. But when the record started playin' I damn near dropped my eyeballs. It was this "Love and Marriage" thing again. But then. This rum-dum, he starts *sing*in' it, croonin' away in this muscatel tenor he's got. Real quick I reached for my drink and I throws it down with a gulp.

Whiskey Bill and Cooper took turns at the cup. Cooper was staring upward, gazing over the wet, slimy wall of the canal lock and then the sheer black riveted hull of the Australian passenger ship, trying without any real hope to get a glimpse of the woman in the white skirt, to see her face, to identify her standing up there, somewhere far above him.

Now, I'm a pretty stout fella and I guess to look at me you might naturally come to the conclusion that I'm slow on my feet or somethin'. You know. Usually stocky guys like me can't jump around as much as some of them skinny guys. But man. Let me tell you. I sure did move fast that time. I was a cross between a kangaroo and a god-damn weasel. Real quick I picks up my foot and pushes over this stool that this Bride of Frankenstein is sittin' on. She goes ass over tea kettle and she's kickin' and screamin' —My *purse!* Gimme my god-damn *purse!* Well. When he heard that, this rum-dum lets out a holler—*I* ain't got your purse, lady! And he jumps up and starts runnin'. *Swish!*

He's right behind me. Now all this only took about a tenth of a second. It all happened in a flash. And I mean. A *quick* flash. This gang of Brooklyn baboons, they're tryin' to get their legs untangled from under the booth. Just about the time they make it, I'm done gone. But this guy with the D.T.'s, he runs right into the middle of 'em, screamin' his ass off. The boys, they lost their heads completely. They thought they had a hold of *me*. Every one of 'em is climbin' over each other to get at this poor guy and get in a couple of good licks.

Whiskey Bill still sat there on the mooring bitt, interrupting himself to look casually around at the scenery. He took a nonchalant puff on his cigarette, his belly jiggling under his billowing aloha shirt as he suppressed a private chuckle.

The gates opened. The *Ocean Endeavor* moved into Miraflores Lake, its stern vibrating as the propeller wash rebounded from the shallow bottom. The ship entered the last lock of the canal system, a two-stage drop to the level of the Pacific. Over the south end there was a very high swing bridge, the intercontinental connection of the Pan-American Highway. The bridge was open. At either end a cluster of automobiles waited for the *Endeavor* to pass.

Anyway. In the meantime, I'm still runnin' for the door like a stri-ped-ass ape and behind me there's all this hollerin' and screamin' and this jukebox is still blastin' away. Well. I shoots through the door and right outside I pretty near runs right over a cop. I was so glad to see *him* I could have *kissed* the son of a bitch. So I grabs him by the arm and I screams—Holdup! They're holdin' up the joint! The cop, he sticks his whistle in his mouth and starts twitterin' away like mad. He reaches for his pistol with one hand and his club with the other and he starts in. Me, I didn't wait. I don't know exactly what happened after that. I was too busy zoomin' around that old corner. But I could hear this fantastic screechin' goin' on behind me.

There's thumps and bangs and hollers and police whistles and the jukebox is still blastin' away with this "Love and Marriage" thing.

Whiskey Bill smirked and squinted his eyes, holding a cigarette in two outstretched fingers.

Anyway. I made it around the corner and after droppin' my keys two or three times fumblin' so bad, I got the side door open and—*swish*. I shoots upstairs to the room. And there's Sleepin' Beauty, all curled up in her birthday suit, snorin' away. I was so god-damn mad I felt like throwin' her right out the window, birthday suit and all. Instead of that, though, I grabbed her by the hair and shook her a couple of times until she finally wakes up. And what's the first thing she says?—*Darling?* What *time* is it? So I yells at her—It's the day of reckoning, sister. Your whole damn family is downstairs. Why the hell didn't you tell me you were the Duchess of the Mafia? So she gets all excited and nervous and starts cryin' and everything. But all she did about it was hold the sheet up in front of her boobs like she was real modest. And she starts whinin' —What'll we *do?* What'll we *do?* But I says—"We," hell. You ain't pregnant, are you? "We" can do whatever *you* feel like. *Me*—I'm leavin'. And with that I grabs my seabag and my suitcase and down the stairs I go. And— bang. I'm through the door and out in the street. But of course. *Naturally*. No taxi. No squad cars. No buses to jump into. *Nothin'*. So I runs around the block like a fiend and finally, after a half hour sneakin' through alleys and hidin' behind garbage cans and leapin' over hedges. *Finally*. I manages to sneak up to the union hall through the parkin' lot in the back. And I goes flyin' through the rear exit and up the stairs to the shippin' floor. Naturally. By that time it was already way past the last job call.

Whiskey Bill let out a great sigh. Getting off the mooring bitt, he drained the cup, making a loud and prolonged sucking noise. He looked ashore, staring at the houses on Diablo Heights.

Well. Anyway. You know the rest. So. Here I am. Like I was sayin'. Between characters like this guy Chico and this Beef Stew Smitty. I never have a god-damn chance. Like I said. You gotta be crazy to be a seaman. They're *all* nuts. Every fuckin' one of 'em.

The final leg of the transit was eight miles long. Several ships were tied up at the docks in the harbor of Balboa. Several more were at anchor. They were waiting for canal passage or waiting for orders, ships with dangerous cargoes or ships needing fuel or repairs. With a roar a launch came alongside to take aboard the line handlers. Then the pilot boat came alongside. Carrying their portable two-way radio and their handbags, the Pilot and the Apprentice clambered down. When the launch was clear, the sailors raised the gangway and secured it for sea. The sun was setting. The *Ocean Endeavor* proceeded out into the Pacific, riding easily in the long, oily swells.

● COOPER WAS STANDING LOOKOUT, watching the trails of phosphorescence made by a school of porpoises leaping and playing just ahead of the ship's stem. There was a fiery green wake, a sudden, sharp gasp of breath and then a heavy splash. Suddenly they all swerved away together. In another moment they were gone, their trails fading out in the blackness of the sea.

Unable to wait for his relief, Cooper faced aft and stood between the two anchor chains, calculating the direction of the wind as he urinated down the hawse pipe. Taking the tobacco pouch from his hip pocket, he filled his pipe, ducking down behind the protection of the bulwarks to strike a match, his face a pale spot, ghostly in the light of the tiny flame flickering in the wind. He was thinking about that other very dark night when he had seen a straight, swift and bubbling green wake in the water. But that one had ended in the explosion of a torpedo. That had happened in the fall of 1943. In October. On the fourteenth. He was sixteen then. Now he was thirty-five. And that meant that his mother, whoever she was, would most probably be about fifty-five years old.

But all that time Cooper and the old bum had been passing the pint of whiskey back and forth, each of them fastidiously wiping off the mouth of the bottle with the palm of his hand and carefully replacing the cap.

Cooper's chest felt tight as he remembered his drunkenness, his screams, his whimpers of pain.

They found me—right where—you're *stand*-ing.

The bum looked down at his feet, nervously shuffling

to one side. He took another pull at the bottle and tucked it under his belt over his stomach. He swallowed. Hesitating, he looked up, his red, dirty face ecstatic.

Like Moses! In the bulrushes! Swept out of the violent currents of the city's *traffic!* Spinning out of the maelstrom of honking horns and squeaking brakes. Taxis. Trucks. Limou*sines.*

The bum cooed with tender sympathy as he led Cooper downtown, crossing Fifth Street and then onto the Bowery, steering him with one arm over his shoulders.

My boy. My boy. Try not to take it so hard. It doesn't really matter. From dust we begin. And to dust we return.

Weaving unsteadily, they went on, the old bum gesticulating with his free hand to punctuate his oratory.

Ah, *yes.* We shall sway and jolt over the stormy seas of this world. Like two lifeboats lashed together. With Captain Mark Cooper at the helm. The Great Navigator. Whose childhood was shiny. Ah, *yes.* But as brittle as glass. Everywhere he stepped, it cracked. And buckled. And cut his feet. His *feet?* Ah, yes. His feet—set in motion by sensitive wounds, sent him marching—*skating,* so to speak, over thin ice. Yes. Until. He slipped and fell. And found himself *gasp*ing. Immersed in the numbing chill and in the *dark*—the somber *blue*—of the SEA!

The bum took his arm away and stopped to raise the bottle to his mouth. Cooper ambled on, swaying and lost.

Cooper's tongue was getting burned at the tip as he sucked on his pipe, tasting the thick nicotine sap. He banged the bowl on top of the mooring bitt, the wind scattering the ashes and fanning them into a glow of sparks bouncing and swirling aft in a brightening, expanding tail. In a few minutes he saw Britt's flashlight coming out of the deckhouse door, advancing in jerks and eclipses over the curving sheer of the deck. He arrived at the bow, his head down, the brim of his dirty old navy cap pulled over his ears.

Well, Britt. Here we are again. Standin' out here in the dark. The rest of the world sloppin' up on that cold beer.

So? We make it all at once. And spend it all at once.

I'm sure glad you're satisfied. I sure as hell ain't. I wouldn't even be on this barge if I didn't happen to pay off last trip in New York. Went on a drunk. And went broke. Every time I hit New York. I always—ah, I—usually go down to the Village. And I always get fucked up.

What's the matter with you? You got channel fever?

Naw. I'm just thinkin'. That's all.

Well. Come on. Eighteen days at sea ain't that bad.

Yeah. I know. Anyhow. Nothin' in sight.

Cooper turned and swaggered aft, his body leaning with the roll and pitch of the ship. In the messhall the coffee pot was perking on top of the small cabinet, held secure by a ring of plywood. He pulled the plug and poured out a cup. Then he sat down, refilled his pipe, crossed his knees and stared at the opposite bulkhead. The Second Cook ambled into the messhall and opened the refrigerator to take out a jar of pickles. He got a fork from the cabinet drawer but forgot the pickles and began to shake the fork at the toaster, scolding it in a low voice.

I had a wagon once. Just like yours. Sure, I did. But the fuckin' wheels came off. And when I talked to him, I told him right straight. Here, George. You take the umbrella.

The Second Cook took a jar of peanut butter from the rack and smeared a thick layer on a piece of bread. Forking out three slices of dill pickle, he laid them neatly on top. Putting a lid on the sandwich, he turned, staring at the open portholes.

Cooper looked at his watch, swiveled the chair around, went into the pantry and poured some coffee into a clean cup. He added milk and sugar and stirred. He went down the passageway and up the ladder to the officers' deck. But as he started for the next ladder he stopped, sniffing deeply as he crossed to the port side, where the smell of smoke was even stronger. He stopped by the Third Engineer's room, put the cup down on the deck and knocked. There was no answer. Sniffing again, he opened the door. He knocked once more and put on the light. The Third was on top of his bunk dressed in his shorts and socks, smoke rising from his pants heaped on a chair. Cooper shook him by the shoulder.

Hey! *Third!* Wake up! Your pants are on fire!

The engineer continued to snore.

Third! *Third!* For Christ's sake, man. Wake *up!*

The engineer mumbled in his sleep.

Yeah. Yeah. Okay.

His pants were piled on the chair with an ashtray in the center. But the cigarette had rolled off and set fire to the crotch and the seat, the web belt already burned in two. Then Cooper saw the dental plate on top of the belt, the flames just close enough to melt it slightly on one side.

Hey! Wake up! God damn it! Your *teeth* are burning!

The engineer snored. Cooper grabbed the pants, the teeth and the ashtray, put them in the sink and turned on the faucet.

So go ahead and sleep. *Sleep!*

Cooper slammed the door.

● WHEN THE FOUR-TO-EIGHT was relieved, they had breakfast and went to their focsle. Cooper sat on his bunk, leaning against the bulkhead, reading a book. Britt lay on his back, blinking up at the mattress sagging above him. Vytas was sleeping on his side, snuggling very close to the doll with his arm around her. There was a knock and the Bosun put his head inside.

You guys wanna turn-to on overtime?

Cooper put his finger between the pages of the book.

*Over*time? You mean Sneaky Pete decided to turn loose?

Yeah. We gotta slush the runnin' gear.

Oh, yeah. Naturally. It would *have* to be some sloppy, greasy-ass job like that.

Well. Overtime is overtime.

The Bosun closed the door. Cooper picked up his book. There was another knock and Watkins, the Ship's Delegate, came into the room.

Cooper? Listen? I got a beef. You're the Deck Delegate. Right? Look. It's about that rubber dummy you guys been fuckin'. Well. The black gang is all pissed off about it.

Yeah? How come?

Well. They figure they should have a turn. We understand why you guys don't want all them Chinks and tree climbers in on the deal. But still—

Britt cut in quickly, raising his head, his face red.

Look. There ain't no discrimination involved in this.

There ain't, huh? You tryin' to tell me that guy Phillips ain't got nothin' against Spades?

Phillips—yeah. But the point is. *We* found that doll. *We* lowered the boat. So she belongs to *us*.

Britt swung his legs over the edge of the bunk.

Look at it from the legal point of view. She was abandoned at sea. A derelict. And we rendered assistance and salvaged her. So we claim her as a prize. Accordin' to admiralty law.

Yeah? Well, I'm glad you brought the subject up. We got a guy. Collins. The eight-to-twelve Oiler. He knows—

Britt stood up, his face redder still.

Clarence Darrow, you mean? Guy's got about ten cases against ten different companies goin' all at once?

Cooper snorted.

Yeah. A real sea lawyer, that guy.

Well. Collins has pointed out that a salvage claim is always divided among the *entire* crew. Not just the deck apes.

Cooper closed his book and tossed it aside.

Look. Don't pound my ear about this. If you wanna go up to the Old Man. Go ahead. Call a ship's meeting if you want.

Britt stuffed his shirt tail down inside his pants, puffing and snorting through his nose.

You ain't gonna get her without an argument. Maybe even a shot in the mouth to go with it.

Britt turned to peer over Vytas' shoulder at the doll. Watkins raised up, his mouth open, his eyes astonished. Cooper leaned back and lit his pipe.

Britt's right. Some of the guys are really hooked on that broad. I mean. Like they're all in love.

Watkins swallowed, his voice croaking.

Yeah? Is she *that* good? How was it? Come on. Tell the truth. Are you really in *love* with her?

Well. Not me especially. I'm funny that way. I like my girls to have warm hands. And a heartbeat.

A heartbeat? Hell, that's easy. We could rig up a little pump. With a few transistors and a couple of batteries. Sparks is real great with electronics stuff.

Oh, my god. Leave it to you mechanics. Always some gadget.

Watkins closed the door, his voice confidential.

Listen, Cooper. Be a little reasonable. I mean. Let a few of our guys get a piece once in a while.

Look. What can I do? I'm only the Deck Delegate.

Okay. Forget it. Maybe I *will* take it up with the Old Man.

The Deck Engineer went out, slamming the door hard. Britt sat on his bunk and put on his shoes. The door opened again. Watkins put his head inside, whispering harshly.

Look. How about rentin' her out, maybe? Just to a few of the guys? We'll settle up first port we hit.

Watkins. If it was only up to me I'd say sure. Fine.

Look. No headhunters. Just a few of the white guys.

Again Watkins left, closing the door softly.

Cooper banged the ashes out of his pipe.

Let's go, Britt. It's time. Hey, Vytas! Let's go.

Vytas raised his head and looked over his shoulder. Ya? Vat's cook-kink?

Let's go. We go on deck. Go work. Over-time.

The Bosun had already mixed up a batch of slush in a fifty-gallon drum in the lazaret. With rags and their bare hands the sailors coated the winch drums and smeared the cargo runners, rubbing the black, sticky stuff into the rusted strands. Other men unshackled the steel blocks from the head of the booms. They dismantled them, wire-brushed the sheaves and the pins, greased them thoroughly and put them back together. Cooper and the Deacon went aloft, climbing the foremast and walking out on the crosstrees with a bucket of tools. They unshackled the topping lift blocks, the weight supported by a two-inch gantline. Waving his scarred, fingerless hands, the Bosun watched the roll of the ship and signalled when to hold fast and when to slack away, the heavy block, the thick topping lift wire and the bull chain all slowly coming down to the deck.

Cooper and the Deacon waited for the gear to be overhauled. They wiped their hands with a rag and managed to light up smokes, each one turning his back to the wind. Leaning against the guardrail, they relaxed, looking down at the other men forty feet below and then looking out over the round horizon and the several hundred square miles of visibility circumscribed around them, open ocean on one side, Mexico on the other, an endless series of ridges and mountains, hot and dry and barren.

Hey, Cooper. Listen. I got a beef.

Oh, come on, Deacon. You too? Everybody's got a beef.

Yeah. But you're the Deck Delegate. Right?

Okay. So? What's the complaint?

How about gettin' my watch partners to lay off me?

What are they doin'? Still givin' you the business because your mother's a church minister?

Naw. That ain't it. What they're doin' is. They're always buggin' me because I won't stick my dick in that rubber whore they're always playin' with. So what law says I gotta fuck a toy doll right in front of a couple guys if I don't want to? I mean. Who's the queer one around here? *Me?* I'm supposed to go apeshit over a *doll?* Otherwise *I'm* the screwball? What is this? Sometimes I think I'm on a funny boat. We're some kind of seafarin' freak show.

Well. This ship ain't so bad. I mean. We got a few

weirdos. But how many ships you been on that didn't? Huh? I mean. You don't really think next trip's gonna be different?

The Deacon looked at Whitey and Reggie working below.

Hell, no. Next trip ain't gonna be different. But I never been shipmates with no *doll* before. Everybody arguin' over whose turn it is. Everybody braggin' about how many times they can come in one night. Everybody comparin' notes on how tight she is. How soft she is. How pretty she is. Whitey and Reggie spend half the time arguin' about what her *name* is. That Whitey now. He's a maniac. I mean it. That bird is *dangerous*.

Yeah. But if Whitey wasn't your watch partner, maybe you'd have Punchy. Or Sanitary Sam. How about old man Britt? I gotta listen to him explain to me every night how he's gonna get rich on the stock market and how this is gonna be his last trip. I don't know. Maybe Whitey ain't so bad.

He *ain't?* And I suppose Reggie is the official mascot for national mental health?

Reggie? He's alright. Seems like a lot of fun.

Fun? Fun? Listen. Let me tell you somethin' about that guy Reggie. I sailed with *him* before. On the *Robin Kirk*. We were in Mombasa. And like. I've seen some performances. But this guy *scares* me. Listen. We were all in the Rainbow one night and there was some Dutchmen in there off some other ship. And one of their guys had a birthday. But it turns out one of our guys had a birthday, too. Same day. So naturally. It turned out to be a happy-birthday singin' contest. And Reggie's jumpin' around all over the place, wavin' his arms and screamin' like a lunatic.

Yeah? Okay. So he likes to have a good time.

Wait. Wait. Next thing I know I looked up and there

he was, comin' through the door carryin' this monstrous *rock*. The damn thing must have weighed two hundred pounds. So, *bam*. He put it on this table and made this great big announcement. This was the *birth*day stone. And naturally. All them stupid drunks, they're cheerin' and hollerin' and pourin' beer all over it. Then they started to pass it around. I'm tellin' you. It weighed two hundred *pounds*. But finally somebody had sense enough to see that somebody was gonna get hurt. So this big ape, he threw it right out the front door. The trouble was. There was this Dutchman outside takin' a piss. He was standin' there half knocked out of his mind when this big, funny-lookin' stone went rollin' past. So he figured somebody must have *lost* it. So next thing I know, I looked up and there's this drunk tryin' to carry it back inside again.

Well. Sounds like you had a swell party. But what's the beef against Reggie? He's a little wild?

Wild? He's crazy. And I gotta *live* with him.

So. If you sailed with him once before. How come you shipped out with him again? I got this job as a pier head jump. But you were on here three, four days before we sailed.

Look. Wait a minute, will ya? Let me finish so you'll know what I'm up against. This rock deal, that was just for warmer-uppers. Next thing, Reggie jumped up and made another big announcement. He said that we were all sittin' in this deep jungle. And it was dark. And there were snakes and flowers and trees all around.

You mean Mombasa? Or East Africa?

No. No. This guy is a *nut*. He meant the *bar*. The inside. Right where we were sittin'. And there was this waterhole right in front of us and all the nice, pretty animals were sloppin' up on all that good, clear water. Yuh got it? It was like the Garden of Eden, see? Then there was this king gorilla. Old King Kong himself. But some mean old white hunters on safari come sneakin' up through the bushes and when he ain't lookin'. They *shoot* him.

Oh, boy. Sounds like a real beer opera alright.

Wait. Wait. So Reggie was gonna be the star of the show, see? And us poor drunk nuts. We're the bad guys. So. Okay. We went along with it. We're cockin' our fingers at the screwball and we're all yellin'—"Bang. Bang." Then he let out this tremendous scream. Oh, Christ. The paint started comin' right off the wall. The bartender was puttin' away all his spare glasses from the bar and Reggie, he's clutchin' his fingers and rollin' his eyes, his face all screwed up like he's in mortal agony. Then he started knockin' over chairs and tables. He was barin' his teeth and growlin' and staggerin' around. He picked up this ashtray. It was just a saucer, really. You know? Picked it up with both hands and took a *bite* out of it. And I swear to *God!* He bit it right in *half.* Then he started wavin' the two pieces around and he was spittin' out cigarette butts in all directions. Meanwhile, all them drunken Dutchmen, they're all yellin' and singin'. And the whores were screechin'—"Bang. Bang. Drop dead, you bastard. It's time for another round." Like, hurry up and die, for cryin' out loud. But Reggie, he was draggin' it out. Down on one knee he went, screamin' and bitin' a table leg. He knocked over another chair, broke a glass and we're all dancin around him, pourin' beer over his head as he's tryin' to grab our feet. *Finally.* Like an hour later. He died. He rolled over on his back with a grunt and just laid there. Then he jumped up with a big grin and took a bow. He grabbed a bottle of beer and started singin' again. Happy *birthday!*

Wow. Sounds like quite a party. But still. What's your complaint? He's a character? What can I do about that?

Oh, for Christ sake. Don't you under*stand?*

No. To tell you the truth. I don't.

This nut. And that *other* nut. They keep tellin' me that *I'm* the nut. Because I can't get a hard-on for a *doll!*

So look. Why don't you just pretend? Take her up in the sack with you. Huh? Pull your jerk-off screen across your bunk. And then just lay there a while and pretend you're goin' through with it. They don't have to know. And she sure as hell isn't gonna *tell* anybody.

Why? Why do I have to go through that kind of malarky?

It was just a suggestion. That's all. Look. You don't really have a legitimate beef. So you can't get along with your watch partners? I mean. I sympathize alright. But you just have to learn how to get along with guys when you go to sea.

Yeah. I know. It's one of the hazards of navigation.

Deacon. Look. I'll speak to 'em if you want. But it'll probably only make matters worse.

Yeah. Yeah. Okay. Forget it. Sorry I mentioned it.

The mast was swinging them through a slow, wide arc with every roll of the ship. The Deacon leaned on the guardrail, flipping his cigarette butt spinning out into the wind. Cooper turned around, scanning the horizon. He thought he could see the spout of a whale a long distance off the port bow. He waited, concentrating on the same spot. In a moment he saw it again, a thin, faintly visible spray. Facing aft, he saw Phillips climbing the ladder to the wing of the bridge, carrying a coffee cup. He saw Punchy come out of the wheelhouse and go below. Then the Bosun yelled up from the main deck.

Hey, you guys! Come on down. It's coffee time!

● THE BOSUN sat on the edge of his bunk, taking a match out of the box by pushing his two ruined fists together and sliding out the drawer with the little finger of his right hand. Awkwardly he rubbed a match against the sandpapered side of the box. It missed fire. He tried it again, succeeded and lit the candle, placing the saucer on top of the cheesebox which had been fastened to the steel bulkhead for a shelf. Pulling off his shorts, he stretched out beside the doll, reaching up to switch off the reading lamp and looking at the eight-month collection of photographs that he had cut out of *Playboy*, *Sir*, *Rogue* and *Male*, pasting them on the bulkhead and on the side of his locker at the foot of his bunk. The nudes were especially attractive in the candlelight, their skin taking on a mystic glow, their faces beautiful in the flickering shadows, each one familiar and beloved.

The Bosun had always been enchanted by fire. And it was fire that had mutilated his hands, had melted them down into the raw, angry shape of eternally clenched fists as he swam through the flames that floated around the sinking tanker. He had been taught what to do at the Maritime Service training camp at Sheepshead Bay, in Brooklyn. Ignoring the rest of the crew and their frenzied attempts to launch a boat directly into a sea of flames, he had thrown away his life preserver and gone over the side. Swimming under water, he splashed away the burning gasoline, clearing an area large enough so he could rise for a breath of air. Again he dove, doing a breast stroke as far as possible before surfacing. Eventually he managed to reach the outer edge of the flames and was picked up by a destroyer escort that had been circling the doomed ship.

The Bosun put his arm around the doll, fondling her breasts with the calloused, scarred nubs of his left hand as he looked at the picture of the blond kneeling on a beach, drying herself in front of an evening campfire. He was thinking of Valerie, remembering the ski resort, that weekend in the log cabin. He was due to ship out. His time limit was over and the Selective Service was threatening to draft him into the Army. But they were lying nude on a thick rug in front of a wide stone fireplace. It was their last night. He turned his head and kissed the doll with dry, affectionate lips. He shifted his weight, supporting himself on one elbow as he rubbed the side of his nose against hers, kissed her and slowly stroked her breast with the thumb of his left hand and with the short, rough and irregular stumps covered with stitch marks and puckered red areas of scar tissue.

The Bosun lowered his head, kissing the nipple of the doll's breast and taking it in his mouth, his fluttering eyelids aware of the burning candle, his own tears, the nearness of Valerie's flesh and by the redness of the night as he drifted closer to the overhead flames. The candle sputtered in a sudden gust of air from the open porthole. The Bosun's hand stroked the doll's Dacron pubic hair, feeling the excess vaseline which had leaked out, melted by the hot water he had poured into her bladder.

● ON WEDNESDAY Captain Pedersen held fire and lifeboat drill. Whitey went to the bow wearing his life jacket. At a signal from the bridge, he rang the ship's bell while the Second Mate was ringing the general alarm, looking at his watch to time the required ten seconds. Mister Teier came up to relieve the bridge. The Second Mate went below to take his station. The crew stretched the fire hoses to the lee side and opened the valves. The engine room was called for pressure on the pumps and five sprays of water blossomed from the starboard side, making patterns of foam trailing over the sea. A moment later the pressure dropped. The hoses were uncoupled, drained and folded back in the racks.

The general alarm and the ship's whistle went off together, seven short blasts and one very long blast—the signal to abandon ship. The crew climbed the ladders to the boat deck, mustering at their stations. Standing on the port and starboard sides, the Chief and the Second Mate called out the roll.

Cooper stood beside the forward davit of number two boat. Beside him was Whiskey Bill, wearing an enormous pair of baggy, knee-length shorts, the straps of his life jacket barely able to reach across his belly. He wore a plaid cap pulled low over his forehead, a rubber werewolf mask over his face.

Raising both hands and crooking his fingers into vicious claws, Whiskey Bill made a spooky howl. He lunged for Sanitary Sam who tottered backward on his short, fat legs, giggling and snickering as he wobbled away in a clumsy retreat. Colliding against Cooper, he giggled again. Cooper flared his nostrils. He was almost certain he smelled liquor on Sanitary Sam's breath.

The Captain watched Whiskey Bill from the wing of the bridge. With slow, resigned dignity, he walked into the wheelhouse.

● VERY CAREFULLY the Deacon laid the doll on his bunk and climbed up after her, pulling across the hanging bedspread. Reggie snickered. Whitey leered.

Well. We was beginnin' to wonder about you.

Reggie sat cross-legged on his bunk and raised one finger as he mocked the stentorian voice of a preacher:

Remember what the Good Book says, my son. For 'tis better to cast thy seed into the belly of a whore than it is to cast it upon the ground.

The Deacon snatched back the curtain.

Aw, come on. The Bible don't say that.

Reggie was immediately indignant.

It *don't?* It don't? You wanna *bet* on that?

Uneasily the Deacon backed down.

Yeah? Where does it say that? What book? What verse?

Never mind. You wanna bet or don't yuh? Huh?

The Deacon closed the curtain again, reaching back to flick off the overhead light. Reggie lay down, grinning.

Just take my word for it. It's in there aw right.

Aw. Leave me alone.

Whitey lowered his paperback sex book.

Yeah. Leave the lover alone. He's got to catch up with his womanizing.

Do you think he knows how?

Sure, he does. He's a real tiger once he gets goin'. Meow. Meow.

Aw, shut up, you guys.

Reggie snickered and made sporadic catcalls for another ten minutes. A little later he began to snore. Whitey fell asleep over his book, his reading light reflected up and around the Deacon's mattress, gleaming on the gloss white paint of the bulkheads and the overhead. Bending his wrist to catch the light, the Deacon looked at his watch. It was 0535. He turned on his side, facing the doll, both of them sliding up and down with the resiliency of the mattress as the ship rolled. Gently he cupped one of her breasts with his hand, then suddenly squeezed it hard with a vicious grip.

Okay, Cynthia. You phoney little bitch. I got your number alright. Floatin' around out there in the middle of the ocean, playin' innocent. Ha. You're about as innocent as a drifting mine. I never could stand whores who bleached their hair blond. Phonies. All of them. Maw is the only woman I ever knew who had *real* blond hair. Standin' up there in the pulpit in her black gown. And her hair like a gold halo around her face. And you jealous bitches run around imitatin' her with your peroxide bottles. Impersonators, every damn one of you. You have fake blue eyes, too. Don't yuh?

The Deacon raised Cynthia's eyelid with his finger. And then he punched her in the stomach. There was a muffled sound of sloshing water. Turning over on his left side, his back to the doll, he rearranged his pillow and tried to sleep. But in a moment his eyes fluttered open, the light dim and blurred, aware of the pale blue pattern of the bedspread hanging beside him, moving very slightly when the ship pitched from end to end. He listened to the repetitive tapping inside one of the metal lockers. Something was rolling, clanking to a stop, then rolling in the opposite direction.

When he was a little boy he would giggle and duck down behind the table, his face against the hanging edge of the pale-blue checkered cloth. Rising, very slowly, the pattern blurred before his eyes as he peeked over the surface of the table, wrinkled and foamed with small white squares. Laughing, he dropped down again to surface slowly and gaze at that bright blond hair and those blue eyes.

Peekaboo! I see you.

The Deacon smiled, taking the bottom of the hanging bedspread and rubbing it lightly over his face. Abruptly he rolled over on his back. This was a phoney cloth with a phoney pattern. Even the color was wrong. It was a Maritime Commission bedspread. Surplus from the war. Couldn't wear the damn things out even after all those years. And he was out there in the middle of the night in bed with a phoney counterfeit female with fake blond hair.

At the head of his bunk was a crude shelf fastened to the iron frame. He dug a knitted wool watch cap from out of the assorted accumulation, an *Argosy* magazine, an ashtray, cigarettes, an open package containing six boxes of wooden matches, a pocket knife and three dusty, corroded pennies. Putting the black cap on the head of the doll, he tucked her long hair under the edges.

That's better. I'll make a brunette out of you. Just for tonight. Keep them phoney blue eyes closed real tight and nobody'll know the difference. You'll look like some plain, honest whore named Cynthia makin' a fast buck. Some black-headed dago hustlin' the waterfront.

The Deacon unfurled the edge of the knitted cap, pulling it down over her face like a black hood.

Better yet. This way the vice squad could never identify you. Oh, yeah. Perfect. Now you're *completely* incognito.

Smiling, the Deacon pulled the doll over, his knee separating her thighs, his free arm wrapped around her buttocks.

If I only had an American flag. I could cover your head with *that*. And fuck you for Old Glory. Anyway.

You can pretend to be the Royal Executioner. Or at least. The Executioner's wife.

The Deacon hugged Cynthia tightly, her breasts flattened against his chest, his face against the rough, scratchy wool that covered her head and face. Slowly he entered her. Pausing to listen to the snores, he began to bite and to kiss Cynthia's breast. He pulled the doll on top of him, then rolled over, Cynthia's back against the curtain. He stopped the nervous jerk of his hips to pull up the bottom of the bedspread and peer out at Reggie, sleeping on the single bunk on the other side of the focsle.

Peekaboo! I see *you*, too. Daddy-o. And I'm gonna get you this time, you crazy bastard. I'm gonna give you a Royal Dose. Like you *never* had before. You'll be reachin' up and yankin' water pipes right out of the bulkhead every time you take a leak. And *then*. In about a week. You'll be shakin' your dick some mornin' and the head of it will fly right *off*.

Grinning, the Deacon rolled over with Cynthia on top.

Yeah, Reggie. You son of a bitch. Guys like you give them whores the clap in the first place. Now you're gonna get it right back. Only *double*.

To keep from laughing out loud, he took Cynthia's breast in his mouth, sucking at it with excitement, squeezing her buttocks with both hands and jerking her hips against his belly.

● WHEN BRITT CALLED the eight-to-twelve watch, Sanitary Sam pulled a pillow over his face and rolled over. Punchy reached for a smoke. Phillips got up and stretched, putting on the multicolored cap he had bought in Mobile. He pulled up his boxer shorts, put his feet into sandals and shuffled out to the head to urinate. But he caught his breath with a sudden, burning pain. The day before, he had been worried about the irritation he felt in the head of his penis. He tried not to remember that his uncle had died of cancer in his prostate glands and kidneys. He knew that too much spice in a man's food can sometimes cause his urine to burn. And the stew the night before had been so bad he had tried to kill the taste with pepper. Perhaps he ended up putting on too much.

At eight o'clock Phillips turned-to on deck. The Bosun had him rig up the Arnesson hammer to start chipping the boat deck. He sat on a wooden box and put on a pair of goggles, turning his cap around backward. Grabbing the end of the thick, flexible cable, he closed the toggle switch on the motor, the cluster of steel knuckles beginning to whir. He bent over, a tremendous racket starting up when the spinning knuckles touched the deck, old paint, dirt, dried fish oil and pulverized scabs of rust rising up in a cloud to dirty his face and his arms. Back and forth he guided the electric hammer, keeping his work squared off, his ears ringing from the noise. But after a half hour, he sat up straight, clutching at his groin. He switched off the motor and went aft to the lazaret to find the Bosun.

Hey, Bos? Listen here. Can ah git relieved? Mah balls hurt me. Awful. Ah think ah got me a strain or somethin'.

A strain? You ain't got the clap, have you? Hell. You can't. We been at sea for more'n a month. Anyway. There's a bucket of paint brushes soakin' in some turps in the mast locker. Take and clean 'em out.

Okay, Bos. Thanks, hear?

Hey, Phillips. You *can't* have the clap. It only takes three days for your pecker to start drippin'.

Phillips slunk away, his head hanging, the Bosun looking at him. But the next morning as the eight-to-twelve was getting dressed, the Bosun stormed into their focsle.

Okay, Phillips. What's the god-damn deal?

What do you mean, Bos?

I got the god-damn *clap!* Yesterday you were moanin' about a strain. A *strain?* You silly bastard. How long you been runnin' around with a leaky dick?

Honest, Bosun. Ah jes started mah own se'f. Yestiddy. Like ah tole you. But listen here. Are you *sure* it's the clap? Ah ain't never had me no gonorrhea before.

I know when I got the clap and when I ain't got the clap.

The door to the twelve-to-four focsle was snatched open and Whitey yelled out into the passageway before slamming it closed.

Hey! What's all the howlin' about out there? For Christ sake. The twelve-to-four never gets no god-damn sleep.

In another minute Whitey opened the door again, wearing a towel and his wooden shower clogs. He glared at the Bosun as he passed, going to the head. But then Whitey's clogs came clattering frantically back around the corner.

I got a *dose!* I got a god-damn *dose!* I started to take a piss and damn near went right through the overhead.

Yeah. We got it too. Me and Phillips.

It's that doll. She's clapped right up to her ears. *That's* how come she was floatin' around out there.

Naw. Come on. Them gonorrhea bugs can't live in salt water. Somebody in the deck gang must have had the clap.

Hey, wait! You sure it ain't one of them nigger bastards in the Steward's Department didn't git into the act somehow? Them niggers *all* got the clap. Hell. They're *born* with it.

Mark Cooper came out of the four-to-eight focsle, smiling and lighting his pipe as he joined the men in the passageway.

Gentlemen. I do believe we all have something in common. Except that I'm luckier than most people. This is my sixth time around.

After breakfast Captain Pedersen left the saloon, exploring his mouth with his thumbnail. There was a crowd of men just outside the door to his office, the Chief Mate in the middle, trying to maintain order, the twelve-to-four Ordinary almost hysterical.

Me? *Me?* What do you mean *me?* *I* never had a venereal disease in my life. I caught it too. Just like you guys. Screwin' that god-damn Goldilocks down there.

The Captain put both fists on his hips and roared:

What's goin' on, here? Mister *Mate?* What *is* this?

Mister Delray was very embarrassed.

Well, sir. It seems that—uh. Some of the men here are complaining that they need some penicillin. They seem to think they've contracted gonorrhea.

GonorRHEa? Oh, Jesus Christ. Just what I need. God damn it. What's next? Mutiny? Black plague? Is this stupid fuckin' rust bucket gonna end up gettin' conked by a fuckin' *whale?* O-kay. O-god-damn-kay. So give 'em a shot in the ass and turn 'em to. No reason why they can't do their work.

Well, sir. The trouble is—

Now, what? What is it? Speak up, man.

The truth is, Captain. I never gave a shot before.

Huh? What kind of a Chief Mate *are* you? Don't tell me you come out of the fuckin' *navy?*

No, sir. But I always sailed on ships that had pursers.

Okay. So now's your chance to learn. Look at all these charity cases. You can start your very own clap clinic.

Well, sir. These pursers. They did all that kind of work. And besides. It would be overtime. I'm off watch now.

Captain Pedersen stood still. The Chief Mate looked down at the deck, at the faces of the sailors and then down again. The Old Man finally spoke with a hoarse incredulous mutter that gradually increased until it was a howl.

*Over*time? Are you out of your mind? Every Chief Mate is in charge of the medicine chest. This is your goddamn *job!*

I'm sorry, sir. But that's not what the Agreement says.

It never fails, does it? God-damn schoolboy mates. Don't know how to do absolutely fuckin' nothin'. But you know what's in the stupid union agreement. Right? Okay. Get me the keys to the hospital. I'll do it myself.

The Captain went below and returned with an armload of supplies. He went into his office, closing the door, the five sailors waiting outside, smoking, fidgeting, glaring at each other. They could hear occasional snatches of song, the Captain's shortwave radio playing music from BBC in London. There were rattles and clatters. Drawers were pulled out and shut. Finally the door opened.

Alright, you guys. Come in here. Line up and show me what you got. Skin it back and milk it down.

The men did as they were told, the Captain going from one to the other, inspecting their organs.

Oh, yes. My, my. That certainly is a sad-looking tear.

The radio was playing Beethoven's "Für Elise." On the desk was a brand-new electric percolator, steaming and gurgling next to a bottle of whiskey and a shot glass. Laid out neatly on a clean towel were several vials of medicine, forceps, alcohol and a jar of cotton balls. The Captain looked at his watch, poured out a shot of whiskey and drank it, closing his eyes with a smile and a grunt.

The men said nothing; Whitey sucking on his mustache, Cooper staring at the bottle of whiskey, the Bosun smoking, Phillips pulling at his cap, the Deacon looking off with a fixed and meaningless smile. The Captain took off the lid of the percolator. Using the forceps, he fished out the barrel of a large syringe and laid it carefully on the towel. He got out the plunger and a total of six needles, lining them up, grinning as the men hung their heads. When the instruments had cooled, the Captain picked up the barrel of the syringe and inserted the plunger, working it up and down. He took a needle by the hub and locked it on the tip of the barrel with a twist, picked up a vial of powdered penicillin, holding it up as he read the label.

Let's see now. Oh, yes. This is real vintage stuff. Charles Pfizer. Penicillin G. Procaine crystalline for aqueous injection. Oh, *boy*.

Captain Pedersen reached for the bottle and the glass.

Let's see. Ten c.c.'s. Three million units. Three *million*. Imagine *that*. But first. Let's have a little anaesthetic.

The Captain tossed down the drink and sighed as Cooper closed his eyes and winced. The Captain pulled the metal cap off the vial of sterile water, soaked a wad of cotton with alcohol, wiped off the top and stuck the needle through the rubber. Everyone watched as he held the vial upside down in front of his face and slowly drew out the ten c.c's of water. The Captain grinned at his silent audience, injecting the water into the vial containing a pinch of yellowish-white powder. Humming along with the piano on the radio, he shook the vial vigorously. Again he injected the needle, drawing out a full load of mixed antibiotic and carefully laying the syringe on the towel. He paused to pour himself another drink.

Okay, gentlemen. Step right up.

The sailors looked at each other.

Come on. Let's not fuck around. Here. You. Step over there by the sink and drop your pants.

Phillips shuffled over, dropping his dungarees and his boxer shorts down to his ankles.

Stand with all your weight on your left leg. Lean on the sink. No, damn it. Keep your arms straight and hold up your own weight. Now. Just relax. Watch this real close, you guys. Who knows? Someday, when you grow up. You might turn out to be a captain yourself. With a crew of clapped-up lunatics. Out in the middle of the Pacific Ocean.

Captain Pedersen slowly ran his fingernail down the center of Phillips' right buttock, grinning when the muscle quivered with a little shiver. Then he drew his finger horizontally, dividing the cheek into four quarters.

Let's see. Maybe I'd better look at that book again.

Taking a thick medical book from his desk, he thumbed through the pages, humming with the radio.

Uh, yeah. Figure 116. The preferred site is—da-da-da—Yeah. Yeah. I see. Upper line along iliac crest—da-da-da—. Okay. I guess I got that.

The Captain held the syringe vertically and pushed the plunger until a fine jet came out. With a cotton ball he swabbed Phillips' behind with alcohol.

Come on. Relax. What's the matter? You nervous? I'm gonna put it in nice and *easy*. Don't worry. I ain't gonna *jab* you. Nothin' like *that*.

The Captain placed the needle against the skin and slowly pushed, Phillips sucking in his breath and flinching. His flesh dimpled, then quivered as the needle went in.

There we go. That didn't hurt none. Did it? And now we'll pull that nasty old needle out. Nice and easy. Real —*slow*. And here's a wad of cotton. All for your very own. That you can wipe the blood off with.

Captain Pedersen turned to his desk, taking off the used needle and twisting on a fresh one. Phillips pulled up his shorts and pants, zipping up his fly and buckling his belt. The Captain poured himself a drink, looking up into Cooper's face for a single penetrating glance.

Alright. Next patient. Oh, by the way. Not that it's any of *my* business. But how do you guys figure you caught the clap, anyway?

Well, suh. We reckon it was Cynthia.

So who's Cynthia? We got one of them girl-boys on board?

She's the doll. The one we found floatin' out yonder.

That dead dummy we stopped for? You guys been fuckin' *that?*

Yes, suh. She's like for real. She really is. Honest.

You don't say? And just how do you terminal mental cases expect me to cure a *doll* of the clap? Huh? Or do you expect to pass it around for the rest of the trip? And just what am I supposed to be around here? A sea captain or a chancre mechanic?

The Captain downed his whiskey. Swiftly, with no hesitation, he jabbed the hypodermic needle into Whitey's buttock right up to the hub. He squeezed in the penicillin, pulled out the needle, wiped off the wound and growled.

Alright. *Next.*

The same five men appeared at the Captain's door the following morning, waiting for their second shot. The Deacon looked around, expecting Reggie. But instead Sanitary Sam and Johan Vytas were there. And so was

Zeke. Inside, they could hear the Captain's radio. The men smoked and fidgeted as Whitey muttered:

Listen. Old Percolator Pedersen's in good form today.

Phillips scowled at the Crew Messman.

Whut the hell you doin' hangin' aroun' up here for? You wont some aspirin or somethin' you come back later. Ain' no nigger on this ship got no call bein' up here now.

Shee-it, man. Ah got me a dose o' clap, too. Ah ain't got no right to git me a shot? Like you whitey bastards?

Whut do you mean by that? You got the clap, *too*?

Ah caught it, too. Tha's all. Like you white mothuhs.

The Chief Cook came around the corner, grinning proudly.

Hang Fang? You *too*?

Me no take. Me pay money go jiggy-jiggy. Me give Sanitaly Sam ten dolla'. Plenny ice cleam.

And then Whiskey Bill sauntered into the crowded passageway, smoking a cigarette held in two outstretched fingers. His belly jiggled as he chuckled, smirking at the others.

Whaddaya say, fellas? What's new?

Phillips jumped for Sanitary Sam, grabbing him by the throat and banging his head against the forward bulkhead.

You *pimp!* You sold her out! You rented Cynthia out to them fat, black, Oriental *creeps!*

Cooper grabbed him by the wrists, putting them away.

Hey, hey, hey. Take it *easy*, man.

Zeke was screeching in a high-pitched voice:

Look, Phillips. Let 'im go. There's 'nough discrimination on this here boat. When we pay off, ah'm gonna bring you up on charges. See if ah don't. Soon's ah see a patrolman.

P*atrol*man. Discrimin-*a*-tion? Look, nigger. Fuck *you*.

Phillips made a lunge for Zeke, who put up his fists

143

on guard, his head bobbing and weaving. Sam rubbed his throat with both hands, whining convulsively.

It was *my* turn. I can lend her to my *friends*.

The office door jerked open and the Captain muttered:

What the hell's goin' on out here? You guys *fight*in' over that thing? Huh? Okay. That did it. I'm confiscatin' that rubber-ass Cinderella. You. Phillips. Go get it.

Why should ah have to—

Go *get* it. *Now*!

Petulantly Phillips went off. The Captain scowled.

Okay, you perverted nitwits. Get in here.

The Captain poured himself a drink, grumbling at the steaming percolator as he took out the sterilized instruments until he was aware that the men were all staring toward the door, where Phillips was holding the doll in his arms. The Captain was flabbergasted, poking a finger into her leg. His eyes grew wide. He pinched her thigh. He pinched the nipple of her breast.

I'll be god-damned. No wonder you guys have gone so apeshit over this thing. For God's sake. She's *real*.

The men began to grin. The Captain jerked.

Put her inside. I'm stoppin' this carnival. *Now*.

Captain? You ain't gonna—throw her over the side?

Never mind. Put her in there like I said. And come back here and drop your god-damn pants.

Phillips put the doll on the bearskin gracing the Captain's bunk. He straightened her legs and folded her hands.

Phillips? Bring that thing back here. Before I hand out any more free penicillin samples, maybe I'd better cure little Miss Mary Maritime first.

You mean—you *ain't* takin' her away from us?

I didn't say that. I'll think about it. Bosun. You and Cooper grab her by the ankles. Hold her up. Higher. Like that. Hold it now while I get some rubbin' alcohol.

Awkwardly the Bosun held the doll's left ankle within the clumsy grasp of his two hands. Cooper was grinning with embarrassment, his chest thrown out, one hand holding up the right ankle, the other hand on his hip. Cynthia hung there, her hair down, her arms dangling.

The Captain returned, looking at the label on the bottle.

This'll kill those gonococcus bugs better'n anything. What I really ought to do is tip *all* you guys upside down. And pour some down your *ass*.

The radio was playing "Claire de Lune." The Captain inserted the neck of the bottle into the doll's vagina and turned it up. The alcohol gurgled and then started to overflow.

Watch it, Cap'n. Don't spill it. It's liable to unglue all her pussy hairs.

Shut up. I know what I'm doin'. I been douchin' out clappy kewpie dolls for the health and sanitation of the Merchant Marine for *years*. Just hold it there a minute and let it soak good. Hold it steady. Alright. Pour her out into the sink. Don't spill it. Bend her legs up. *Bend* 'em. That's it.

Whitey was delighted, grinning at the other spectators.

Hot damn. I done seen all kinds of douches in my time. I mean like—vinegar. Lysol solution. Chlorophyll— oh, that one used to be real great. But this is the first *hootch* douche I ever did get to see.

The Deacon giggled.

Yeah. I'll bet it smarts, too.

AFTER SUPPER Cooper went from room to room to inform all hands about the special meeting of the Deck Department. Quietly they gathered in the Bosun's focsle, sitting on the bench and the two bunks or standing around the room leaning against the bulkheads, arms crossed over their chests or hands in their pockets, smoking, picking their teeth. When everyone had arrived, Cooper started.

Listen. The Bosun wanted to call this meeting. Because. Today he had a talk with the Old Man.

The Bosun looked around the room, glancing at Vytas.

Why don't Vytas go up and relieve Britt? Just for the meetin'. Half the time he don't dig what's going on anyway.

Vytas looked at his watch partner, confused.

Vat? Vat he spik?

You go wheel. Man come down. Ten minute only.

Ha? Hokay. You vant I go up stair. Ya?

The Ordinary went out. Again there was silence. Men smoked and licked their lips, dug fingers into their ears and stared out the portholes at the sea. In a few minutes Britt arrived, solemnly taking off his Navy cap.

The Bosun began:

A while ago. The Old Man called me up to his room. And he said we been havin' a lot of trouble on the ship on account of that doll. And he wants to put a stop to it. In *fact*. What he wanted to do was throw it over the side.

The Deacon began to whine.

That's what he ought to do. That's how come we found her floatin' around out there. Full of clap and everything else. Like somethin' fell from outer space.

Well. As far as I'm concerned. I think she's pretty hot stuff. But let's get to the point. I had a hell of a time doin' it. But I talked the Old Man out of the idea. What's been goin' on is, the rest of the crew has been bitchin' like hell. And the thing is. Pedersen wants peace and quiet on his ship.

Whitey stepped forward.

Peace and quiet? On his pretty little yacht? Huh? Why don't he see to it we get some decent chow?

The Bosun wearily shook his head.

Let's not go into that. Huh? I mean. That's another argument. The fact is. *He* is the Captain. *He* thinks that *we* are causin' dissension among the crew. So *he* decided to throw our sweet little Cynthia right over the fuckin' side. So *I* talked him out of it. But only on one condition: We gotta decide on which man is gonna own the doll. Right now.

What about everybody else?

Everybody else is shit out of luck. Because if *one* man owns her. Exclusive. There won't be no more arguments.

Whitey walked to the door, lighting a cigarette.

Then what? He's gonna have the guy *marry* the girl?

Look. If you guys don't like the idea, then we'll just give her the deep-six.

Everyone looked at each other. Cooper spoke up:

The Bosun's right. We're lucky. We're gettin' a break.

Whitey looked down at the deck.

Okay. So what do we do? Cut cards? Or cut throats?

Cut whatever you want. Cooper? You got any ideas?

Well. I guess we got to have some kind of a draw. Phillips suggested:

We could have ourselves an anchor pool.

Britt sneered.

We won't be at anchor for three more weeks.

The Bosun sighed.

Look. It's simple. We just pull a number out of the hat.

Reggie began to get excited.

No. Hell. Wait a minute. Let's make a sporting proposition out of this. Let's use the distance we run from noon to noon. We take the number of miles. And we just use the last number. From one to zero. What's the matter with that idea?

Whitey made a face.

It ain't worth a shit. There is only ten numbers. Right? But we got eleven men. Ten *here*. And one on the wheel.

The Boson sneered.

Ah. That noodnik. He wouldn't know the difference anyway. He can't even understand what you tell him.

Cooper was indignant.

Vytas? He's a damn good worker, Bos. You got no squawk.

Aw right. So he can work. But I got to pick him up and point him right *at* the job. And put the tools right in his hand.

Well, still. He's entitled to a full chance. Besides. He was on lookout. You get right down to it. He's got a better claim than anybody else here. He saw it *first*.

Until then, the Carpenter hadn't said anything.

Well. You don't have to count me in. I'm too old for playin' with dolls. I got my god-damn dignity to think about.

Cooper bit his lip. But the Bosun was eager.

Okay, then. You guys satisfied? We got ten men. And

nobody can get the Second Mate to fudge on his sextant. First he's gotta shoot the sun. Then he works out the sight. Gets the latitude and puts it on the chart. Right? Then he lays down his ruler from noon to noon. Draws a line. And gets the course made good. Right? And *then* he whips out his dividers and steps off the distance. So he can't know himself until the last second. Cooper? You wanna draw up the list? I got some paper in my locker. And a pencil.

Cooper took out the writing pad and wrote down the names.

So who's gonna get what number?

I want seven, muttered Sanitary Sam, pouting.

Anybody object? Alright, Sam. You got seven.

Gimme three, said Britt.

I'll take number nine, said the Bosun.

Whitey leered, amused by this new game.

Gimme—uh—*eight*. For a date with fate.

Reggie was peeved.

Hey. *Please*. I thought this idea up. How about a chance here? Like four? The number to score with the whore?

Cooper tried to get everything clear.

Tomorrow's the day. Agreed? From noon today to noon tomorrow. And we use whatever figure the Second Mate writes up in the log book for distance made good. No changes. No arguments. No appeals. No beefs. Each guy has got a number. Whatever gets put in the log book is *it*. It's official. The winner gets Cynthia. Lock, stock and asshole. Everybody else keeps his hands off.

How about Vytas? What about him? asked Britt.

He has to have zero. That's the only number left.

The Bosun stood up.

Okay, you guys. The meeting's adjourned.

● AT APPROXIMATELY 1511 HOURS, the ship crossed the 180th meridian, the international date line. That night the clocks were retarded one hour but the calendar was advanced one whole day. Instead of the next day being Sunday and a day of rest, it would be Monday, a work day. All that night the deck gang reacted with various forms of anticipation and bravado, the personal quirks that signified their expectations to win or their preparations to lose. Some talked too much, some were silent. Whitey relieved Reggie on the wheel by shouldering him away and growling:

Gowan. Scram. You lousy number four. Let a genuwine, bona fide, real-live number *eight* take over.

Holy jeez. What are you? A poet?

That's me. Eight the Great. Beat it. Four for nevermore.

Since Cooper held a license, he suddenly became the deck gang's consultant on celestial navigation. When he mentioned the subject of "personal error," they were agog with the possibility that one of the mates could be wildly inaccurate with his sights due to some congenital flaw in his eye.

Phillips began asking the Third Mate all sorts of questions. But he answered only with meaningless grunts, propped up against the forward bulkhead of the wheelhouse, his shoulder wedged against the frame of the porthole box, braced against the roll of the ship. Phillips persisted. Finally Mister Teier went outside on the starboard wing, where he leaned on the wind dodger, looking through the dull green glare that loomed out into the night, pretending to maintain the standard posture of silence of an officer on watch.

The Second Mate had already relieved the Third and was bent over the table in the chart room when Reggie came in with a cup of coffee.

Good evenin', sir. How's it goin'?

Huh? Oh. Hello, Reggie. Fine. I guess.

The Second Mate went back to the log book where he was making out the customary entry, printing the names of the lookouts and the helmsmen during his watch.

Uh. Hey. Mister Mate? Listen. How many miles do you think we'll do tomorrow? By noon, I mean.

How should I know?

Well. You're the navigator. Guess. Take a guess.

But how do I know what kind of wind we'll get? And what kind of current? Here. Today we made two hundred and twenty-five point four miles. That was for a twenty-four-hour day. Okay. That gives us an average speed of, nine point three nine knots. But we retard the clocks one hour tonight. Right? So if we go the same speed for twenty-*five* hours. That makes two hundred and thirty-four point eight miles.

Reggie pursed his lips and stared at the figures scribbled on the back of an old copy of Notices to Mariners.

Point eight, you said? You measure it to the *tenth?*

Yeah. Always. I like to keep my work accurate.

Aw. Well. Okay. Thanks a lot, Mister Mate.

Reggie turned to go into the wheelhouse.

The Deacon was on lookout, wondering what he should do if he suddenly became the owner of the doll. He looked up at the sky, thinking that if it were overcast at noon, there might not be any sun for a sight. Whitey was in the messhall on standby, looking into his coffee cup and thinking about Cynthia. The day men were already in bed, the Carpenter on his side snoring, the Bosun lying awake, looking at the images pasted on the bulkhead, barely visible in the faint glow of the moon and the reflection from the masthead light.

The next morning the Third Mate was nervous and distracted. He had never navigated in east longitude before and had half forgotten the formulas memorized by heart in the examination room. Every day he had had the habit of subtracting the Greenwich hour angle from his longitude in order to find the meridian angle. But now that he was in east longitude, and had to *add* the GHA to his longitude and then *subtract* the total from 360. Before he realized his mistake, he had been entering the H.O. 214 book with the wrong t-angles.

Phillips was relieved early. Whitey came in at a quarter to twelve with his broad leer, his head tilted back, his bushy mustache stretched wide by his grin.

Hey, man. What the fuck's goin' on?

Christ. That gawd-dam' Third never tells me nothin'. Here. The wheel's amidships. She's steady on two-five-six. Takin' some right wheel. Couple of spokes.

Okay, Dad. Two-five-six. Right between the anchors.

Phillips went into the chart room, stretching his neck to see what the Third Mate was doing. He gave the course, heard it repeated and then went below, squeezing through the crowd at the foot of the ladder and in the starboard passageway, waiting, smoking, but none looking at each other. One of the firemen sauntered by.

What's goin' on? You guys all waitin' for a bus?

No one answered. The Fireman became uncomfortable, sidled past and went to his room, looking back once and wondering.

When the Second Mate finished writing up the noon report, he knocked on the Captain's door, went in and gave him a carbon copy of the slip. He crossed over to the port side and gave another copy to the Radio Operator.

Then he went into the wheelhouse and gave the last copy to Whitey.

Here. Take this down to the Chief Engineer. Did real good today. Made nine point sixteen knots.

Yeah? *Yeah?* But what was the *dist*ance?

Two hundred and twenty-nine miles. Exactly.

Exactly? You mean, two two nine point zero? *Zero?* Oh, shit. God damn the stinkin' luck.

Whitey grabbed the slip and stormed away, not bothering to give the mate the course or returning the wheel to midships. Flustered, the Second began to steer, easing the wheel rapidly when he realized that the ship was using too much rudder. Instead of going down to the Chief Engineer's office, Whitey ran down to the main deck, where the deck gang was waiting. Cursing violently, he waved the noon slip in the air.

It's *even*. It's *even*. It's nothin'! Who's got zero?

What do you mean, it's even?

Two two nine point zero. Here. See? Two twenty-nine. *Exactly.* I gotta go back topside.

The Bosun snatched the slip away, holding it wedged between his two fists. Whitey grabbed it back and ran up the ladder, his curses heard until he was out of sight. Everyone was quiet until the Bosun spoke aloud, his voice desperate and wheedling.

Listen, Cooper. I had number nine. Right? That means I win. Two two *nine*. I won. She's mine.

No, it don't. The *last* number, we said. That's a zero. This Second is a nut for accuracy. Works out a Mercator sailing every day with logarithms. He gets his miles to the nearest *tenth*.

Who said anything about tenths? Last *number*, you said.

Come on, Bos. You know what we meant. He even wrote it out with a zero at the end. It's Vytas who wins.

Vytas? That half-pint foreigner? He don't even know what we're talkin' about. The dumb bastard don't even care.

Everyone turned toward Vytas, who stared back, looking solemnly up at Cooper, at the Bosun and then at the others.

Nope. You lose, Bos. By a tenth of a mile. If it had been two twenty-eight point *nine*. Then you'd have won.

The Bosun stared at the men, but everyone looked away.

One tenth of a mile? That's a cable length. Hardly much more than the length of this ship.

Yeah. If we'd been just a couple minutes slower. If the wind had been just a little stronger. Well. You know.

Reggie said:

Cheer up there, Bosun. I'm just like you. I been too far ahead of myself all my life.

What are you? Funny or somethin'?

Well—Jesus Christ, Bosun. Don't take it so hard.

Don't be such a fuckin' wiseguy.

The Bosun went into his room. He unhooked the door and slammed it shut. The men stared. Gradually they turned toward Vytas. Nervously he looked back.

Hey. Vat's cook-kink?

You win, Vytas. The doll is yours.

Ya? She be mine girl frent? Ha? You spik troot?

Yeah. Come on. I'll take you up to the Captain and tell him that you're the lucky man.

● ON THURSDAY Vytas was the man on lookout when the sky began to lighten and become pale, the stars disappearing in the morning twilight. Vytas could see the Chief Mate on the wing of the bridge with his sextant and his stopwatch. He turned and waved his arm. Vytas waved back and began walking aft. When he went into the messhall, he found Cooper reading a book. The Second Cook was banging oven doors and pots, preparing to bake bread for the day and to start breakfast. Vytas called the Chief Cook and then went aft to the messmen's focsles. Rapping on the door, he went inside, flicking on the light switch.

Hey. You guy. Six clock.

Whiskey Bill flinched, putting his hands over his eyes.

Hey! Put that light out.

Vytas flicked the switch off. He hooked the door open and left. The Saloon Messman was lighting up a cigarette when Plip Plop, on the bunk above Bill's, called down:

Oye? Que hora e'?

Sei' hora', was the mumbled answer.

Whiskey Bill rubbed both eyes with the heels of his hands and swung his legs over the side of his bunk. He sat there, his chest wheezing as he moaned. Then he heaved his bulk upward, pulling his pants up over his belly and staggering to the bench to flop down and put on his shoes. Grunting, he sucked at his teeth.

God-damn Latvian lunkhead. "Hey you guy six clock." Couldn't get nobody but foreigners to take this fuckin' job. We oughtta be flyin' one of them monkey-country flags. Yakkety yakkin' all day. You'd think the shitnoses would learn to speak American. Six o'fuckin' clock. What a stupid time to get out of the fart sack.

Plip Plop dropped down lightly from the upper bunk, got dressed and went out to the head, his sandals making their characteristic noise. Whiskey Bill lurched out into the passageway, his arms upraised and his fingers lightly brushing against both bulkheads as he made his way to the pantry for some coffee. He dropped heavily into one of the chairs in the old gunners' mess, across the table from Cooper. He slumped with a dejected scowl. Neither of them said anything until Cooper sighed.

Jesus. What a life.

Whiskey Bill didn't answer.

I mean. What a way to make a livin'. Huh?

Silently Whiskey Bill sipped his coffee.

Ah. What I probably should do is go get myself married. Or something like that. You know. Get a job ashore someplace.

Without moving his elbow from the top of the table, Whiskey Bill moved his hand and head to take a very short, absent puff on his cigarette.

I was married once.

Cooper picked up his cup and drank. He swallowed. Then he glanced at Whiskey Bill, waiting.

Well?

Huh?

So. What's the story?

What story?

You just said you were married once. Okay. That one must be good for an hour and a half. At least.

Whiskey Bill glanced up quickly into Cooper's eyes. Again he puffed on his cigarette. He placed his thumb against his right temple, his fingers dangling loosely over his face. Cooper watched him. Softly he asked:

So? What happened!

Uh. Nothin'.

Whiskey Bill made a slight shrug with his massive shoulder. Huskily, he added, almost in a whisper:

She died.

Cooper looked at Whiskey Bill for several seconds, then looked away. For a long time they sat there. Neither of them moved. Neither of them said anything. They could hear the Messmen in the pantry getting coffee. Spoons clinked. Cups rattled. One of the rotating seats in the messhall banged against the edge of the table. Zeke started to tell about the rumble he once had in Formosa when three Chinese detectives came up to his hotel room in the middle of the night, angry at the way he had filled out a government form for the desk clerk. Under the question, "Purpose of visit" he had printed in bold letters—

FUCKING.

● THE BOSUN WENT BACK to the fantail and knocked off the Carpenter. Whitey was spot-chipping the bulwarks just aft of the house, banging away with a hand chipping hammer.

Hey, Whitey! Coffee time!

Whitey looked up and snatched away the goggles, letting them dangle around his neck as he wiped the sweat and the particles of rust off his face with a rag. The Deck Engineer and the two Wipers came up from the engine room, laughing and talking as they lined up behind the sailors in the pantry. Stamas, the four-to-eight Fireman, came in rubbing his eyes. He poured some coffee, stirred it and dropped the spoon into a glass of water. Zeke came in, gave a brief, sullen stare at the crowd and took his cup back to his room. Collins, the Oiler, was freshly shaved, his hair wet and neatly slicked down flat. He looked around at the sweating, bare-chested men wearing dirty dungarees and greasy caps. There was a pair of work gloves lying on the deck, half the fingers with holes worn through. Reggie's shirt was torn between the shoulder blades and the knees of his pants had been repaired with big stitches of waxed sail twine.

Christ. You guys look like a bunch of hoboes waitin' around for the next freight. Hey, Whitey. What happened to you?

Somebody's got to work around here, Dad. We can't all be big-time sea lawyers.

Oh, I don't know. When it comes to bullshittin', you

got real talent. Come on. Tell us another one of them lies. How about when you used to be pimpin' down in New Orleans?

Naw, Dad. You don't wanna hear that old jazz again.

Well. Tell us how come you're so bad. I mean. You gotta admit. You're pretty bad.

Oh, yeah. I'm bad alright. I'm so bad I'm scared I'll get a finger bit off whenever I wipe my ass.

Several men guffawed as Whitey ran a hand through his long blond hair and rearranged his West Coast cap down over his right ear. He sucked at his teeth. He puckered his upper lip with its bristly mustache and stuck out his chin.

Cooper and Vytas came into the pantry and reached for coffee mugs, the crowd suddenly silent, looking away, uncomfortable. Cooper took a seat. Vytas sat across from him. The messhall was quiet. Cooper looked into his cup and then at the other sailors as he drew on his pipe. The Bosun turned his face away. Whitey stared at the end of his cigarette. The Deck Engineer squirmed in his seat, his jaw muscles tight. With narrowed eyes he looked at them all.

Look, you wise-ass deck monkeys. Maybe you think this is my first trip. Huh? Let me tell you somethin'. I happen to be an old-timer in this union. And I know a lot of the patrolmen back in New York. So now what's this shit about you guys havin' a lottery for the doll and nobody in the crew knew anything about it? Huh?

No one said anything.

A secret lottery? What kind of a fuckin' democracy is this?

Cooper spoke up:

We drew lots. And Vytas won. So that's it.

That's *shit*, you mean.

Look. Go ask the Old Man. He don't want no more

dissension. He read us the riot act and gave us a direct order. So we did it. Johan Vytas here owns that doll. It's his.

Vytas looked around the silent room at all the faces turned his way. He sipped his coffee. The Bosun sucked in his lips, pushed them out, pulled the lower one in between his teeth. With both his nubbed hands, he picked up the cup and set it down.

Asshole luck. That's all. I came within one ship's length. One lousy tenth of a mile. All that stupid Third Mate up there had to do was blink his shit-eatin' eyeballs. Just once.

Watkins was furious.

What are *you* bitchin' about? The rest of the crew didn't even get a chance.

So. How do you do it, Vytas? Huh? I mean. You stick needles in little images or what? I mean. You come from some wild-ass country back there on the other side someplace. Right?

Vytas looked at the Bosun and then at Cooper.

Lay off him, Bos. It was fair and square.

What d'ya mean? I'm just talkin' to the guy. What's the matter? Can't have an ordinary conversation around here?

Whitey laughed and then sneered at the Bosun.

What are you lookin' for? Sympathy? Only place you'll find *that* is in the dictionary. Between "shit" and "syphilis."

You stay out of this. I'm talkin' to Vytas. I got a right to talk to a guy, don't I? So? What have you got to say for yourself, Vytas? Nothin', huh? Boy. You and that kewpie doll make a good pair alright. Mister and Misses Dummy.

Vytas raised his cup, his eyes shifting to look inside.

Yeah. The Silent Squarehead. But I remember one night he talked, though. Back in New York. I'm about the only guy still on board, see? I'm sittin' right here in the messhall. All of a sudden. In comes the Dingleberry Kid. All tanked up. Tie crooked. Shirt messed up. Hair flyin'. And he's tellin' me this big long story about this waitress he picked up. Oh. He's *talkin'* alright. He's foamin' at the mouth. With this Lower Slobbovian accent he's got. All about how he took this broad to a restaurant and he's fillin' her full of booze and swishin' her all over town in taxis. But *then*. He takes her home and tried to get into her pants. But she looks at him and says. But wait a minute. This is how *he* said it, see?

The Bosun went through a staggering pantomime.

He's standin' right here in the middle of the deck. Swayin' back and forth. His eyes are all out of focus. His mouth hangin' open. And he says that this waitress broad told him—"Vat? You tink am whore? You vant fock first *night?*"

Vytas looked at the Bosun with a slight smile. The other men roared. Phillips laughed with a convulsive cackle and leaned toward Vytas, glancing at the Bosun for approval.

Hey, Vytas? Is that whut she said? Sure 'nough? "Whut you think? Ah'm a whore? You wanna fuck the first night?" Is that right?

The Bosun grinned.

Yeah. That's just the way he said it. Three sheets to the wind. Broke. Out of his mind. With this crazy accent. "Vat? You tink am *whore?*" And he rolls his r's, see? He says "whorrrrrr."

Everyone laughed. The Bosun smiled, looking at the clock.

Okay you guys. Let's turn-to. When you come out at four o'clock, Vytas, I got some winch beds that need cleanin' out. You can start at number one hatch. Crawl under and scrape out all the grease and crap. And chip away any rust you find.

Vytas glanced at Cooper, confused.

Explain it to him, Cooper. And you go and relieve Whitey.

Hey? Are you serious? Are you really gonna make him clean out winch beds?

Hell, yes. I'm serious. He ain't got no beef. You four-to-eight guys only put in an hour a day on deck, anyway.

But what kind of asshole job is that?

Never mind. I want it done. And I want *him to* do it. So explain it to him. He's your watch partner, ain't he?

At the door, Reggie turned and looked back at Cooper.

Hey. It ain't three-thirty yet. But you're called.

From outside in the passageway, Whitey mimicked:

Hey. Nov Shmoz Ka Pop? You vant fock first night?

● AFTER HE WAS RELIEVED on the wheel, Vytas came down to the messhall. The Second Cook was chewing on a peanut butter and pickle sandwich as he hung his head, looking down at the deck. Vytas got some coffee and sat down. The Second began growling.

Them bunch of phonies. I was a deckhand myself, once. We're goin' up the Mississippi, see? And I'm on the wheel. And the Pilot, he says, "Steady as she goes."

The Second Cook stood up, his fingers curled as though holding the spokes of a ship's wheel.

And so I says, "Stea*dy*."

Vytas sipped his coffee. The cook's lips curled.

But then the lookout called up the bridge on the telephone. And the Captain answers it. And the lookout says, "Hey. I got my leg stuck out the porthole. What'll I do?" And the Captain. He says, "Aw. To hell with it. Tell him to use his own god-damn mosquito net."

The cook stood there, his arms out, his fists clenched. Then he rammed the end of the crushed sandwich into his mouth, bit off a chunk and sat down, slamming his back against the swivel seat and scowling down at the deck.

Vytas finished his coffee and went to the four-to-eight focsle. When he put on the light, he saw that the bedspread carefully tucked in around the doll's body was now disarrayed. Her arms and legs were not in the same position and the bathrobe was wrinkled. He unfastened the robe, cautiously running his hand down between her legs, stiffening when he felt the stickiness.

Vytas began to whimper, his chest heaving with a deep, uneven twitch when he saw that the nipple of her left breast was gone, a small, rough hole torn out of the artificial flesh. With a mournful groan, he stepped back from the bunk and beat his forehead with both fists. But then he saw a small object on the deck. He picked it up and held it in the light. It was the doll's nipple, the back of it a torn white surface of foam rubber, the front molded, smooth, pink and brown, the teeth marks plainly visible. Vytas stood there, the tears running down his cheeks. Again he whimpered, shutting his eyes tight, leaning his forehead against the pipe frame of the bunk as he sobbed:

Mara—Mara—Mara—Mara—Mara—

He straightened up, snuffled his nose and wiped his eyes with his sleeve. He examined the nipple in his hand and carefully put it in his pocket. Working quickly and with purpose, he stripped the doll and carried her out to the Deck Department head. He placed her buttocks in the sink so her legs were vertical, propped up against the bulkhead. Her arms dangled, her head squeezed between his knees. Vytas worked up a lather with a cake of Lava soap, washing out her vagina and rinsing it several times as he cursed and moaned under his breath.

He dried the doll off with a bath towel and carried her back to the focsle, placing her on his bunk. He stormed out into the passageway. Pausing to spit at the door of the Bosun's room, he stamped his way aft to the eight-to-twelve focsle and leaped inside with a booming yell:

Hokay! You hate tvelf. Ha? You come go vatch.

Phillips lay on his bunk reading the *Reader's Digest.* Gawd dam', boy. You're a mite early, ain't yuh?

· Come. Drop sock. Go vatch. No bull-shit.

Punchy raised his head drowsily, groping for the switch to the reading light. Vytas slammed the door and ran up to the ladder to bang on the door to Mister Teier's room.

Up in the wheelhouse the Chief Mate was leaning in the porthole box staring forward. The moon was almost on the meridian, bathing the deck in a strong light. He saw the circle of illumination from Vytas' flashlight moving jerkily along the deck toward the bow.

Relieving the lookout a little early, isn't he?

The Mate stiffened and reached for the binoculars.

What the hell's he got with him? My god. It's that *doll*. He's bringing it up to the *bow!* Listen, Cooper. I can't have a man standing a lookout like *that*. I mean. Let's face it. You could hardly call that standing a proper lookout in a seamanlike manner. Him up there playing dolls.

Well, sir. You gotta make a few allowances for Vytas.

Why? I'm *always* making allowances for seamen. But they never make any allowances for *me*. That's for damn sure.

Yeah. But he's had it pretty tough. His English is pretty wild. And he don't talk much. 'Less he has to. Or maybe if he's real mad. But he's from Latvia someplace. And during the war his whole family got knocked off. First the Russians took the place over. Then the Germans came in. And then the Russians came back again. I don't know the details. But he's been fucked up from the word go. He's like. Well. You know.

But look at him. Sitting up there on the bow. With his arm around a naked woman! I mean—a naked *doll*.

Yeah. Calls her Mara. Must have known a Mara once.

Well, look, Cooper. You're the Deck Delegate. And you're his watch partner. And besides. You always sort of look after him, don't you? Big-brother stuff and all that?

Well—you know. You see, Mister Mate. I'm an orphan. Well. A foundling, anyway. And. Way I figure it. Hell. I might even be related to the guy. I don't know. Poor prick. He ain't got nobody anywhere. Can't even talk to nobody. So—

Look. Tell him for Christ sake. We don't need any figurehead on this ship. Right? A nude love goddess carved on the bow would have been just great back in the old days. But not now. Tell him that. *Please?*

Yes, sir. I'll try to make him understand.

Look. He can smoke on lookout. Recite shithouse poetry. He can even doze off if I don't know about it. But no friggin' in the god-damn riggin'. That's too much.

Yes, sir.

● SANITARY SAM jerked open the door to the wheel-house, short of breath and peevishly whimpering.

He called us too early.

Who?

Your Ordinary. He called everybody at a quarter after. We're not supposed to be called until seven-thirty.

Yeah, Sam. I already *know* that. Did he check the time?

He knew alright. He knew. He was just mad, that's all.

Yeah? Well. I'll speak to him about it. Okay?

Cooper slapped his hand against the king spoke.

She's all yours. Two-five-two. Two-five-two, Mister Delray.

Sanitary Sam repeated the course and the Mate echoed it. Cooper took the empty coffee cups and went below. When he got to the focsle, Britt was seated on the bench, one shoe already off.

Hey. What the hell's wrong with Vytas tonight?

Beats the shit outta me. I think he' blown his stack.

The steel storm door slammed shut outside, the dog handles dropping. There was a rustle of rubber and Vytas came in, wearing his slicker and carrying the doll in his arms.

Bastit Bosun. No fockin gut some bitch.

Hey, hey. Take it easy, Vytas. What happened?

Vytas shifted his burden, reached into his pocket and took out the doll's teat, holding it out in his hand.

Some bitch. She fock op. See? See?

Cooper stared, not really understanding, delicately pushing up the doll's left breast to examine the jagged wound.

Somebody—somebody *bit* off her—tit?

Ya. Ya. Some bitch Bosun bastit fockin hell shit.

Easy, now. Easy. You'll wake up the whole ship.

You fix? Ha? You fix gut?

Cooper looked at the tears rolling down Vytas' face.

Yeah. I think so. I'll try. Sure, why not? Chips has some Elmer's glue in his room. That stuff will fix anything.

Vat you say? You fix gut? Ha?

Yeah. Yeah. I fix. You stay here.

Cooper went out. The door to the Bosun's room was closed. In the messhall, a hand of pinochle had just been finished, the players rapidly counting their points.

Chips? Can I use some of that Elmer's glue you got?

The Carpenter shifted his quid with his tongue.

Yeah. Okay. Deal, somebody. I'll be right back.

Cooper followed the Carpenter to his room. Before going in, he knocked sharply several times and then waited. The Bosun was reading an old *National Geographic* magazine, his knees raised, the covers pulled up to his chest. As Chips took the hasp of the padlock out of the handle of his locker and opened it, Cooper realized that Bosun hadn't once put down the magazine, that he was lying there stiff, almost without breathing.

Back in the focsle Cooper stretched the doll out on his bunk and adjusted the reading light. Vytas hovered nearby. Britt sat on the bench, both shoes off and his pants dropped down to his ankles. Cooper squeezed the plastic bottle, smearing the wound in the doll's breast with a generous amount of glue.

Britt began to mimic in falsetto:

Doctor Cooper. Surgery. Doctor Cooper. Surgery.

Come on, Britt. Knock it off. This is serious.

Vytas glared.

Ya. No sink dirty stoff, you.

Cooper smeared more glue on the reverse side of the mutilated nipple and carefully replaced it, pushing hard to establish a good contact between the opposing surfaces.

Damn. How the hell do you clamp a woman's tit?

Well, Doctor. Whenever I have similar difficulties, such as getting caught in a wringer? Or bending over too fast while I'm ironing in the nude? Welllllll—I find that I get best results with Johnson's Band-Aids.

Hell, yes. And you got a box right in your locker.

Britt resumed his normal voice, croaking hoarsely:

Yeah. But I *need* them. Case I cut myself or somethin'.

Come on. Gimme a couple. It won't hurt yuh.

Britt got out the Band-Aids. Cooper applied two of them, crisscrossed in a tight X over the injured teat.

There. In a couple of hours the glue will set up and it'll be stronger than the other one. Might be a little harder. Or stiffer. Like a scar, maybe. But it'll hold.

You fix gut. Ha?

Yeah, Johnnie. Operation's a success. But you better take it easy tonight. Huh? You sleep. Mara sleep. Tomorrow okay.

Vytas tenderly hoisted the doll up to his bunk. Grinning, he nimbly climbed up and slid between the sheets. He gave Cooper another smile and pulled the curtain closed. Cooper winked at Britt. He went out to return the glue to the Carpenter, came back and muttered in a low voice:

That Bosun *did* do it. Vytas is right. I can tell.

Cooper undressed, got into his bunk and turned on the shortwave radio, tuning the dial until he got some Japanese music. He cut off the speaker and adjusted the headset over his ears. He relaxed, feeling drowsy, aware of the roll of the ship and the weight of his own body shifting on the mattress.

Britt was already in bed. Beside him was a pile of

back issues of *The Wall Street Journal*. With slow and profound study, he worked on the looseleaf notebook of charts. He lettered a series of X's and O's to signify the ups and the downs of the market's fluctuations, very careful to fill the printed squares of the graph paper in an orderly, neat manner. He examined the chart of the stock he had just brought up to date. He turned the page. Again he looked at the columns of figures in the *Journal,* the opening sale, the high, the low and the closing price. He considered. Lightly he made a single, tentative mark with a pencil. Then he turned the page to the following chart.

Cooper glanced at the flat pale blue and gray of Vytas' curtain. He watched Britt as he worked with methodical enjoyment, then turned his back, snuggled down, smiled and closed his eyes. He fell asleep with the earphones still in place, thinking of the woman in the white skirt going through the Panama Canal, aware of the motion of the laboring ship as he listened to the fragile, quavering voice of a Tokyo geisha singing an Oriental favorite.

● COOPER BEGAN the morning watch by taking first wheel, relieving the Deacon, who lit a cigarette and inhaled deeply.

That fuckin' watch partner of mine, Reggie.

Deacon? *Again?* Why don't you two get married?

Wait. You don't understand. I really *know* this bird.

Look. How come you keep shippin' out with him?

You don't understand. It just *happened* to me, that's all. I came aboard and *pow!* There he was. But wait. Listen. Last night he was talkin' and moanin' in his sleep again.

Hell. Everybody does that.

Wait. Listen. One time me and him were on this Isthmian Line C-3 on the Far East run. But they got strict prohibition in Bombay, see? Really dry. So we went ashore and we bought this homemade booze from one of the broads. Twenty rupees for a quart. It was made out in the country. Outta plum seeds. Like slivovitz. But this stuff was on the weak side so they jazzed it up a little. They pulled out the cork and poured in a little ether.

Ether? Hell. That'll kill yuh, won't it?

Naw. It was regular operatin' room ether. But *man!* Three or four drinks of that stuff and you're climbin' trees. As a matter of fact, that's what Reggie *did* do.

The Chief Mate came into the wheelhouse, the Deacon's story trailing off in embarrassment.

Yeah. That Bombay run. I mean. To hell with that Isthmian outfit. Anyhow. I'll see you later.

Cooper studied the lighted segment of the gyro repeater showing the lubber's line and the course numbers. The ship rolled and pitched, the gyro clicking constantly. Shortly after two bells the horizon began to lighten behind the ship. Mister Delray stood on the port wing, aiming his sextant, measuring the altitude of the star Betelgeux. He snapped the button on his stopwatch and scurried through the wheelhouse to the chart room. At five-fifteen Britt came up.

Okay, old buddy. Steerin' two-five-zero. Looks like it'll be a clear day. Sun'll be up in a few minutes.

Yeah. I know. Rises in the east. Pisses me off.

You're not mad at the sun, *too,* are yuh?

Not the sun. This fuckin' ship. This fuckin' company.

Better than no ship at all. And that ain't so far off.

It ain't that. It's this idea of goin' the wrong *way.*

Oh, shit. Are you still hung up on that?

Here. I got *proof.* I got the Mate to let me look in one of them books that give the distances between ports? Huh?

Britt unbuttoned his shirt pocket and took out a folded piece of paper on which were written various ports and their distances in nautical miles.

See? From New York to Panama. Huh? And then straight over to Manila. Okay. Grand total: 11,519 miles. *But.* Get this. If we had gone the *other* way. *East.* New York to Gibraltar. And then to Port Saïd and through the Suez Canal. Then Singapore. Huh? Okay. And then from Singapore to Manila. Total? 11,491. That's twenty-eight miles *shorter.* That's the right way. *East.* Every morning we should be lookin' that sun right in the fuckin' eye.

Britt. Look. It costs about fifteen hundred bucks a day to operate one of these old Libertys. And twenty-eight miles is no more than four hours' steaming time. At the most. That's one sixth of a day. That's two hundred and fifty bucks' worth of time. But maybe the Suez Canal charges a lot more than the Panama Canal. Then there's the different prices of fuel to think about.

You're makin' the same mistake everybody else makes. You're *assumin'* that since this is the way we're goin' that automatically makes it the *right* way.

Look. I don't really give a shit. Either way is okay. Here. Steerin' two-five-zero.

Cooper went below. At 0600 he called the Steward's Department and then went to the cleaning-gear locker. He filled a bucket with hot water and carried it up to the bridge. The squeegee and the rags were kept in a drawer under the settee in the wheelhouse. A Turk's head brush and a mop were stuck behind the oxygen breathing apparatus. When he finished cleaning the portholes, he quickly swabbed down the decks. He emptied the bucket over the lee side, filled his pipe and lit it. Leaning against the bulkhead to imitate the Mate's habitual posture, he whispered hoarsely to Britt:

Steer a good course now, Quartermaster.

Aye, aye, sir.

They both grinned.

Hey, Britt. Did you ever hear of drinkin' *ether?*

Ether? Yeah. Gives you a real bang. But we ain't got *nothin'* on this tub. Not even plain, ordinary shellac.

Shellac? Sure we do. We got lots of shellac on board.

We do? Where?

Cooper came closer to the wheel, his voice low:

Back aft. In the lazaret.

We do, huh? *Hey.* What do you say we make up a batch of Kickapoo Joy Juice? Have ourselves a little *party?*

Do you know how to strain shellac and all?

Hell, yes. Canned heat. Sterno. De-rail. All that stuff. Trouble is. The Bosun keeps the lazaret locked up.

Tiptoe into his room and swipe the key. Whenever I call the day men the two of 'em are always out cold. And see if you can get some bread out of the galley.

Okay. I'll get the stuff. Meet me back aft.

After he was relieved by Vytas, Britt went back to the fantail and found Cooper waiting with two loaves of bread, two clean gallon jars and a gallon can of shellac. Hoarsely they whispered with giggling excitement as they pried off the lid with a marlin spike, Britt sniffing with expertise and pleasure.

Oh, man. Grade A. The best. Smell that bouquet.

The ship's bread was heavy and coarse and unsliced. Britt tore at one end with his fingers, digging out a scooped cavity. Placing the other end on top of one of the jars, he balanced the loaf vertically as Cooper slowly poured the shellac into the hole.

Careful now, man. Don't spill it. Easy. Here it comes. Yeah. It's startin' to come out. See how clear and clean it is? All the gum and resin stays behind in the bread.

Cooper threw the empty can over the rail. It landed on top of the following swell, hesitating, following the ship for a moment and then spinning away in the foam, diminishing into the distance of the boiling wake. Cooper sailed the lid overboard to skip off a wave, skitter and sink, glittering like a coin in the deep blue of the sea.

Squeeze it a little so we don't waste nothin'.

Oh, man. Look how *clear* this stuff is.

Britt went to the taffrail, dropped the soggy loaf over the side and began pulling a handful of bread out of the end of the second loaf. They repeated the process. When the last of it had been poured in, Britt waited, giving the loaf a gentle squeeze and watching the final rivulet drip through. Quickly he stood up and threw it over the side.

Climbing over the deck cargo, they went forward, on the alert for anyone loitering around the house. Sneaking in through the starboard door, they slipped into their focsle.

Better dog down that porthole. And the storm cover.

Man. Breakfast cocktails! Just what we need.

How about we jazz it up a little? Maybe I can swipe some orange juice out of the messhall.

What we *really* need is some lemon extract.

Hey! We got some Aqua Velva. How about that?

Cooper sneaked out of the focsle and into the mess-hall, taking a can of breakfast orange juice out of the refrigerator. They poured the quart of juice into the jar. Britt added in a half bottle of after-shave lotion. He screwed on the lid and shook the jar gently as Cooper stood by with the water glasses. With a flourish Britt poured. He put down the jar, smiling. Cautiously they sipped, shuddering violently.

Say. Listen. How 'bout we invite old Whiskey Bill to come in for a snort?

That guy? Are you kiddin'? He's a maniac.

Aw, come on. He's just a good-hearted slob.

But once he gets in here he'll talk our ears off. He goes the first fifteen minutes without even breathin'. It takes him two hours just to get his second wind. And after *that!* Christ!

Yeah. That's true. But not always. Sometimes he—

Cooper was silent for a moment, looking down into his glass.

Anyway. You gotta admit. He never tells the same story twice.

Well. Okay. But still. *No.* Okay?

They sat on their bunks, Cooper holding his glass up to the light and peering through it with one eye shut. Seriously they sipped their drinks, grinning bravely. Britt leaned against the bulkhead, reclining into the semi-darkened cave formed by the bunk above him, the bedspread and the towels and dungarees draped over the ropes. He felt behind him and pulled out his chart book, replacing it with a pillow.

Tell the truth. How much stock you own in this company?

Me? Are you serious?

Come on. You been goin' to sea steady for thirty years. Hardly no time on the beach. You must be loaded.

Maybe. Maybe not. I've had my losses, too. Even now the market's not doin' so good. Sixty-one was a good year. But sixty-*two!* Wow! Anyway. I wouldn't be caught dead with steamship stock. This is the most depressed industry in the country. We got international competition, man. Anybody that can carry a crate of blivets from point A to point B cheaper than the next guy. He gets the business. And Americans just can't keep up.

You mean, union wages and all?

Wages. Taxes. Coast Guard regulations. Obsolete ships. Interstate Commerce stickin' their noses in. Foreign-aid gimmicks. Phoney subsidies. Controls. Let's face it. This is strictly boom or bust. And it only booms when there's a war goin' on.

So how come they stay in business?

Got to. Just like us. They don't know nothin' else. Inefficient bastards. If they had any real brains they could compete alright. Automated ships. Containerized cargo. Even atomic power. But. Well—look right here. Christ. They're runnin' *this* ship halfway round the fuckin' world in the wrong *direction.*

Oh, shit, Britt. Are we back on that again?

Cooper drained his glass, shuddered and grimaced.

We'll both be stone cold dead by tonight. Drinkin' this stuff. Tastes like triple-distilled dog shit.

Cooper reached down for the jar. Britt leaned forward and held out his glass. Cooper poured, turned on his radio and sipped his drink, looking up at the doll on Vytas' bunk, covered with a sheet.

What we need now is a little Japanese music. And some female companionship. Shall we invite Cynthia to join us for a cocktail? I mean—Mara. Or whatever her name is.

Sure. Tell her, come on down. Join the party.

Cooper stood up and uncovered the doll, placing her

in a sitting position beside him on his bunk. One arm around her waist, he raised his glass with his left hand.

Here's to the ladies. Long may they fornicate.

They both drank and shivered.

Hey, Britt. What do you suppose she was really doin' out there? I mean. Like. Where did she come from?

Some other ship, I s'pose. Got thrown overboard.

Yeah. I guess. Unless it was some kind of a secret Communist conspiracy. Just to bug the American Merchant Marine.

Anyway. If I ever figure this fuckin' stock market out, I'm gonna go ashore and buy myself a half dozen *real* dolls.

Cooper began to sing, waving his glass:

> *I'm gonna buy a paper doll*
> *That I can call my own.*

Britt joined in.

> *A doll that other fellows*
> *Cannot ste—eal.*

They broke up, took another swig and went on.

> *And then those flirty-flirty guys*
> *With those flirty-flirty eye-eeees—*

Cooper turned and kissed the cheek of the doll.

Give me a kiss, baby. Admit that you can't *live* without me. You can't even sit up straight without me supportin' you.

Give the lady a drink. What kind of a gentleman are you?

Cooper put the glass to the doll's lips and tilted it

up, filling her mouth. He bent her backward, leaning over to give her a long, loud, slurping kiss. Sitting up, he made a comical face for Britt, looking cross-eyed and shuddering.

Wow! When *this* broad kisses. Man—you *stay* kissed.

Britt cackled. Turning his head with mock prissiness, he imitated a female voice:

Oh, you men. You're so *dirty*-minded!

Cooper mimicked in the same female tone:

You speak for yourself, Mary. You're just jealous.

Jealous of *you?* You shameless, nude hussy. Don't be ri*dic*ulous! Those silly boys may think your shit don't stink. But us girls. *We* know better.

As he laughed, Britt fell back against the bulkhead with a bang. Cooper bent over, holding his middle as he roared. He reached for the pickle jar, filled Britt's glass and then his own.

Here. You drunken old South Street fart.

Cooper broke into a quavering imitation of an old woman:

I keep telling you, son. *Please*. Don't keep hanging around with those seamen. They're just bums. Drunken *bums*.

Britt growled with contempt:

Aw, fuck you, Maw.

They both spilled some of their drinks, snickering uncontrollably. Cooper picked up the doll and held it by the back of the neck, moving her head like a scolding woman shaking with fury.

Oh. I should wash your mouth out with soap. You naughty child. And after all the things I've done for you.

Britt fell back against the bulkhead, waving his hand.

Aw. Drop dead, Maw.

Oh. *Oh*. My own flesh and blood. Oh. Ohhh*hhhh*. My heart!

Cooper let the doll fall forward in a heap on the deck.

Good riddance. Damned old bag. Buggin' me all my

life. You're a lucky bastard. You never knew your old lady, did you?

Nope. Never made her acquaintance. She was too busy doin' crossword puzzles and hustlin' for her beer to pay any attention to a shitty little *bastard* like *me*.

Is that the way they *really* found you? In a *beer* case? On a street corner?

Yep. That's me alright. Washed ashore. Just floatin' through the traffic in my own little cardboard boat.

And there wasn't no way at all to identify you? No toys? No note? No bottle? Nothin'?

Sure there was. It was a Ballantine's ale box. The guy that ran the Foundling Home. That's where I grew up. He wanted to name me John Ballantine. But some of the sisters got upset. So they settled for Saint Mark Cooper. On account of they found me across the street from Cooper Union. In Greenwich Village. At the corner of St. Mark's Place and Third Avenue. But then they decided to knock off the saint part. They figured I didn't really qualify for that.

Britt frowned for a moment and then muttered:

Ah. You're lucky, man. You just don't know.

Sure I am. Hell. I got adopted. Three times as a matter of fact. Until they gave up on me. Besides. I had parents of real distinction. My mother was an intellectual. They found me all wrapped up in the Sunday *New York Times*. And the crossword puzzle was completely filled in. In ink. It was green ink. And get *this*. There were no mistakes. Not one.

I still say you're lucky.

Yeah, I know. Look at it this way. I'm not related to nobody. Right? But that means I *could* be related to *any*-body. I could be a Catholic. Or a Jew. I could be Irish. I could be a Swede. A Russian. I could even be Latvian. Like Vytas. Hell. I might even be his nineteenth cousin or somethin'.

Man. You just don't realize. I had a mother. Wow. But my old lady was *noth*in' compared to my sister. What a bitch *she* was.

Britt growled down at the doll sprawled at his feet.

How you doin', Sis? Ha? Cat got your tongue? *Fin*ally?

With another falsetto, Cooper imitated a female voice:

Ouch. You're hurting me. You brute.

Yeah? How about all them times you and your girl friends used to beat me up? Huh? Right in front of the other kids?

Britt picked up the doll and held it across his knees, spanking its bottom harder and harder until he stopped, grinning, out of breath and triumphant. With a flourish he held up his glass, his little finger stiff and sticking out. He drank, his expression smug. Cooper sat up and tried to control his laughter.

Ladies? And *gentle*men! We are honored tonight with the presence of that international. Roving. Seagoing lover. Mister—Randolph—*Britt!*

Britt smirked. He picked up the doll and set her beside him, one arm around her shoulders, purring gently:

Oh, my dar-ling. I 'ave miss you all zose lone-ly ni-ights at sea. When I stand on look-out an' see all zose miles of oceans aroun' me. All I see are your beaut-i-fool eyes. Lak ze stars in ze sky. Dar-ling. Spik to me. Tell me zat you luf me.

Cooper imitated the voice of an enamored girl.

Oh, Randy. When you touch me I just tingle. All over.

Keess me. My sweet. My dar-*ling!*

Oh, yes. *Yes*. But first. How about twenty bucks? For a short time? I mean—just to help with the rent?

Cooper fell back on his bunk, laughing, his legs kicking in the air. Slapping the doll with the back of his hand, Britt tossed her on top of Cooper, her hair flying, her limbs sprawling loosely. Cooper wrapped his arms and his legs around her body and began to growl. Britt was singing, his voice thick and slurred:

> *When I come home—at ni-ight*
> *She will be wait-ing—*

There was a rap on the door and Phillips came in, blinking, confused. Cooper growled as he kissed the doll. Britt went on singing.

Hey? Whut's goin' on? You guys didn't call the watch.

> *She'll be the truest dolly*
> *Of them a-a-a-a-llll—*

Hey. Knock it off a second. Huh? Shit fire. It's a damn good thing ah was awake and saw whut time it was. But how 'bout the Third Mate? Yo'll gonna call him or whut?

Britt waved his arms and touched his heart.

> *I'd rather have a paper doll*
> *To call my own-n-n-n*

Jesus. Hey? Whut's that stuff yo'll been drinkin'?

You want a snort? Here. Help yourself.

Phewwwww. Not *that* stuff. What the hell *is* it?

Number one, Grade A, one hundred and ninety proof, bottled in bond, genu-wine, imported—shel*lac!*

Shellac? You done gone nuts? That stuff'll *kill* yuh. Anyhow. Ah'll go an' call the day men.

Don't forget to call your old buddy, Mister Teier.

Wrinkling his nose, Phillips closed the door.

When Punchy relieved the wheel, Vytas went below. But he stopped outside the door when he heard voices inside the focsle.

> *A doll that other—felloooooooows*
> *—Cannot—ste-eallllll—*

And Vytas heard another voice, female and hysterical:
Oh, no! Don't make me do that! Not *that!* PLEASE!

Vytas snatched open the door and leaped inside with a howl, both fists clenched and at the ready.

Mara!

The unhooked door swung back and forth with the uncertain roll of the ship. The room was quiet except for the lilt of Japanese music on the radio. There was a lurch to port and the door slammed shut. Cooper and Britt sat on their bunks, grinning up at Vytas with pleasure, their faces red, delighted and stupefied. The doll was sitting on Britt's lap, hugging his neck. He supported her with one arm around her back, a drink in his hand, the other arm over her thighs.

Oops. Looks like we got caught, Mark. Old Johnny boy got us with his wifey. Red-handed. Red-assed and everything.

You *Nazi* guy!

Aw, come on, Johnny. We were just havin' a little fun. Come on. Have a drink. This is *real Liebfraumilch,* this stuff.

Vytas knocked the offered drink out of Cooper's hand, the glass crashing on the deck. He stood there looking down at him, his fists clenched, his jaws knotted, his eyes wide.

Vat? You drink dirty stoff? You sink dirty stoff, too? You steal *vife?* You—you Nazi guy. Ya? You like Nazi guy?

Cooper sat there, stunned. Britt didn't move. Vytas grabbed the doll out of his arms, jerked open the door and went out. Again the door swung back and forth with erratic movements as the ship pitched and rolled until finally it slammed shut.

● WHISKEY BILL finished his coffee and went up to the officers' deck. He got his gear. He filled the bucket from the faucet in the head and carried it into the Chief Mate's room. He went back for his push broom, the mop, the fox-tail brush, the dustpan and the cardboard box he used to collect his trash. Bill closed the door and went over to the bunk. He pulled up the foot of the innerspring mattress and took out a bottle of whiskey that had been wrapped in a towel and wedged against the springs. He unscrewed the top, took a long drink, shuddered and made an ugly face. He replaced the cap and put the bottle back.

Blinking his eyes and shaking his head, Bill pulled out the wrinkles of the bottom sheet and tucked the edges between the mattress and the wooden sides of the bunk. He pulled up the top sheet and the green officer's bedspread and skillfully poked down the edges all around. He dumped the contents of the two ashtrays and then the wastepaper basket into his cardboard box. He polished the mirror on the medicine cabinet over the sink, using a dirty bath towel. Sprinkling Comet in the sink, he wiped it out with the opposite end of the same towel. He paused to look in the mirror, felt his whiskers, examined his teeth and sneered at himself.

Yeah. What a way to make a livin'. Floatin' around out here. No broads. No bars. No god-damn TV. Nothin'. Nobody to talk to but a bunch of screwballs. So dumb you could beat their brains into a gnat's ass with a tack hammer. Like that deal with that fuck doll they fished out of the drink. That nigger bastard Zeke is right. There *is* discrimination goin' on against the Steward's Department. Just because most of the guys ain't white. What he don't realize is, they're discriminatin' against me, *too*. Hell's fire. *I'm* white. How come I got cut out of the picture?

When he finished mopping the deck, Whiskey Bill moved all his gear to the First Assistant's room, pausing to look at the card fastened to the door with the name Thomas Frederick Horton, an address in New Jersey and a telephone number. Bill went over to the bunk, the bedspread only slightly wrinkled, a round depression in the top pillow. He grinned.

Yeah. Old T.F.H. Twenty-Four Hours. Never sleeps *in* the bed. Just on top. Goes all day and goes all night. Scared he'll miss somethin' and not get the Chief's job. Filthy son of a bitch ain't been out of his clothes in a month.

Bill pulled up the end of the mattress, took out the bottle of whiskey, opened it and took a long swig. He wiped off his mouth and put the bottle back, jamming it tight.

Yes, sir. *Mister* Harrison. That was a smart move. These old Libertys may be old and they may be slow. But the passageways are narrow. And there ain't no private heads for each one of the fuckin' officers. For an old-time professional B.R. like you, man. Nothin' like it. Work two hours a day if you know how to do it right. Except on Fridays when you gotta change the linen.

Whistling between his teeth, Whiskey Bill cleaned the mirror. He grinned, crossed his eyes, pouted his lips and imitated a goldfish. Squinting, he coyly examined his three-quarter profile. Going up to the next deck, he rapped very lightly on the door to the Captain's office. He waited and then crept inside until he could see that the bunk was empty. When he was sure that the Captain was not in the head, he reached under the mattress for the bottle, took a drink and put it back. Peeking out the porthole, he saw Captain Pedersen on the boat deck doing deep knee bends.

His tattooed arms were held straight out as he went down, the bald spot on the back of his head showing pink, the wind blowing his lavender shorts tight around his small, thin buttocks. Bill sneered, pulled back the foot of the mattress and had another drink. When the bed was made, Bill picked up the heavy polar-bear rug from the settee, mumbling as he unrolled it on top of the bunk.

God-damn rat hide. Got to get it just right. Turn it so the face aims straight for the office door. Son of a bitch got no right to make me play around with his god-damn personal toys. I'm the B.R. I make the beds, swab the decks, keep everything clean. That's all. What am I? Chief butler in charge of the god-damn trophy room?

Bill looked at the fixed snarl of the mounted head, the teeth bared, the nose wrinkled, the eyes squinted.

Grrrr. You must be his brother, you hairy-ass monster. What I'd like to do is skin *him* and stuff *his* head and aim it right for the front door to scare everybody with.

Bill bent down, his hands on his knees, staring closely into the bear's glass eyes. He bared his teeth and growled.

Grrrrr. Rowwwwwwww—rrrrr!

Whiskey Bill! What the hell you doin'?

Bill jumped, grabbing the mop handle and feebly moving it over the deck, harking and clearing his throat.

Nothin', Captain. Just singin' to myself. That's all.

*Sing*in'? Singin' what? "The Bear Went Over the Mountain"? You're *drunk*. That's what. Ain't you? Come on. Admit it.

Cap'n Pedersen. *Please*. I keep *tell*in' you. I do my share o' drinkin'. Yeah. I'll admit that. But only when I go ashore.

Yeah? I suppose you *always* throw a bucket o' water over the windward side. Huh? Like the other day? And it blew right back in your face? And you were already so god-damned soused, you didn't even notice?

Captain. I ain't got nothin' to get drunk *with*. You already searched all my gear and stuff. Right?

I know. I know. You got it stashed. Real good. I gotta admit. But if I ever do manage to find that whiskey, I'm givin' it the deep six. And you with it. You hear me?

Yes, sir. The Articles says, "No grog or sheath knives allowed on board." But I ain't got no grog or no sheath knives.

Grog, shit. It's *booze* I'm talkin' about. Git outta here.

Yes, sir. Soon's I swab out the head.

Never mind the head. Just scram outta here.

Yes, sir. Okay. Right away.

Impulsively Bill tugged at the bear's foreleg and dusted off the top of its head, giving it a loving pat. He grabbed his mop and broom, dustpan and brush and took them outside. Coming back into the office for his cardboard box, he reached under the desk for the waste basket and dumped it. As he was leaving, the Captain stopped him.

Hey! *Wait* a minute. Just a god-damn minute.

Yes, sir?

Captain Pedersen gave Bill a sharp look and stared down into the box half filled with trash. Bending over, he stuck both arms into the pile of waste paper, cigarette butts and orange peelings, groping back and forth, his fingers scraping the bottom. Whiskey Bill had a bewildered look as the scowling Captain stood up and dusted off his hands.

O-kay. Be on your fuckin' way.

Yes, *sir*.

Bill went outside. As soon as he turned the corner, he grinned, imitated a goldfish, turned toward the Captain's door and snarled silently, baring his teeth and curling his lip.

● BEFORE GOING BELOW to the saloon for breakfast, the Chief Mate washed his hands. He was running a comb through his hair when the Ordinary appeared in the doorway, holding the naked doll in his arms, sputtering with his fury.

Hey. You Met. You vant look-out no voman. Ha? You vant go vatch gut. Ha? You planty smart some bitch. Vy you no gif lockem op hancoff? Some bitch no steal?

What? What did you say?

Lockem op hancoff. No steal. Eferytink hokay.

Did somebody steal something from you?

Steal Mara. Take vay I go vheel. Fool roun I vork.

Somebody took you—uh—girl friend. Right? And you want me to what? Lock her up? Don't you want her?

Ya. Ya. I *vant*. Hancoff better. Fixem some bitch.

Captain Pedersen was in the head, shaving. His radio was on very loud, the BBC orchestra playing the "Hungarian Rhapsody." There was a knock on the door of his office. Swearing, he came out into his bedroom, completely naked, his face covered with lather.

What the hell you want, Delray?

Sir. Vytas here has a complaint. Seems that some of the crew have been molesting his doll while he's on watch. He brought it up to the bow with him one night on lookout. But I stopped that. I didn't want my men not keeping a good lookout.

Yeah. So? What's wrong with that?

Well, sir. Now it seems that the men in his own focsle are fooling around. You said that the man who won the

doll was supposed to have it as his own personal property.

So what the hell am I supposed to do now? Put her
in the ship's safe? Those bums keep fuckin' around down
there and I'll chop her ass up and make erasers out of her.

Well, sir. Vytas figures you made him a promise. And
right now he would like to borrow your handcuffs.

The *hand*cuffs?

Yes, sir. If he locks up her hands to the frame of his
bunk, he figures nobody can abuse her.

Hands? Hell, that's no good. What he *really* needs is
a chastity belt. Tell you what. Call down to the engine
room. See if you can bullshit one of them shade tree auto-
mobile mechanics down there into makin' him one. Be
careful now. No overtime's involved for *this*.

Yes, sir. That's a good idea, Cap'n. I'll see what I can
do. But until then. Can he use the handcuffs?

Yeah. Take 'em and get the hell out of here. They're
in the top drawer of my desk on the left. If he loses that
fuckin' key, I'll keelhaul the idiot. Give him whatever he
wants. Give him one of the pistols. Give him a flare gun.
Give him the Lyle gun. Maybe he'll murder about two-
thirds of the crew for me. But whatever you do. Get *him*
and get that *doll* the hell out of here. And let me *SHAVE!*

Yes, sir. I just thought it would be good relations——

Fuck their relations. Fuck 'em *all*.

Yes, sir. Sorry to disturb you, sir.

● WHITEY AND REGGIE turned-to on deck, each carrying a can of paint, working together just aft of number four hatch. They were catching the places around the two storm doors in the mast house where all the blisters of rust had been taken down to the bare metal with chipping hammers. Someone else had already scraped and wire-brushed the spots and put on a prime coat of red lead. Now they were putting on a second coat, a little white paint added to differentiate the color.

The Bosun was standing behind the mast house by the starboard winch, wondering if he should replace the runner or wait until after they discharged cargo at Manila. He had only four extra runners on the ship. If they were to be diverted to some other ports, it might be several months before they took on any new deck stores. The Bosun rubbed his nose with the stump of one of his amputated fingers. He took a drag on his cigarette, stepping over one of the turnbuckles that secured the deck cargo to the padeyes on deck. He stood on the guard that protected the steam line to the winch, kicking at the crumbling scabs of rust and mill scale.

Reggie was laughing just around the corner of the mast house. Whitey was growling with his half-facetious snarl:

Hey, man. I'm beginnin' to miss that bitch Cynthia.

Yeah. She was a pretty good lay alright. Even if she was a little stupid.

Whitey put his brush into the paint pot, took off his work glove, lifted his cap, scratched his head and pulled the cap down over his right ear. Reggie worked in his usual nervous style, his brush moving very quickly. The Bosun started to come around the corner of the house but stopped when he heard himself mentioned. Reggie was giggling.

I guess that four-to-eight Ordinary is havin' a real ball. I wish it had been me that won that doll pool.

You wish? Every swingin' dick in the deck gang wished. Especially that Bosun. He went absolutely *queer* for her.

Yeah. He turned purple when he found out he was only one number away from winnin'. I think the goofy bastard's in *love* with that thing. I really do.

So's Vytas. So's everybody else.

Yeah. But with the Bosun it's different. I mean, he's really *serious* about the girl. And then that goofy Lower Slobbovian Ordinary had to go and win her.

Well. That's the way the pussy pisses.

Reggie tittered.

Just when I was beginnin' to get used to gettin' laid regular. Now I gotta go back to jerkin' off.

At least you got hands that you can jerk off *with*. What about that slob Bosun? He has to jerk off with his *toes*.

Reggie danced around in a little circle, stamping his feet with hilarity.

Oh, man. Can't you just see him? Goin' into a cat house someplace to get himself a *toe* job?

As ugly as he is. He'd probably have to pay a hundred bucks even for *that*.

Reggie saw the Bosun just as he made one more turn of his slapstick dance. Hissing to Whitey, he dipped his brush into the pot and bent down low to smear red lead on another spot. Scowling, the Bosun stood there, his knuckles on his hips.

Hey. You guys need any more red lead?

Naw, Bos. We got enough.

When you relieve the Deacon on the wheel, tell him where you were workin'. Have him take over where you left off.

The Bosun turned toward the house with a slow, rolling swagger.

That night after supper the Bosun took a shower, put on clean shorts and lay down on his bunk, the back of one hand resting on the bridge of his nose. His eyes fluttered, blinked, closed and opened. But he would always be able to see the watery blackness of the sea at night and a red smudge blazing above him as the flames floated around the sinking tanker.

Holding the cigarette with his little finger against the adjacent nub, he brought it to his lips, inhaled deeply and slowly let out the smoke. But he also saw the smoke being exhaled by the whore in the back room at Gracie Woodyard's place in Port Arthur. Her back was turned. She had pulled her slip up to her armpits, paused to take a drag on the cigarette and place it in an ashtray. Then she pulled the slip over her head, speaking over her shoulder:

You wanna unhook me, Sugar?

Arthur Touhy came closer and took his hands out of his pockets, trembling as he touched the woman's back, working his little finger and his thumb under the brassiere strap and trying to pull them together. The cloth slipped and he tried it again.

Splashing away the burning high-octane gasoline, he had cleared an area large enough so he could rise for a breath of air. Again he dove, swimming through the black and the red and the pain, trying to go as far as possible before surfacing and putting his hands up into the fire, before choking down his own scream, gasping for air, returning to the black silence below.

Come on, baby. We ain't got all night.

Again he fumbled, his hands quivering. The woman

turned around, impatient and peeved, her movement so quick his hands were still raised just below her face. With a start, she sucked in her breath. He stood there, looking into her staring eyes. Then he turned and left, kicking the door in anger when his two sweating palms slipped on the tight porcelain doorknob and he had to twist it the second time.

The Bosun swung his legs over the side of the bunk, sitting up with a quick jerk. He slipped his bare feet into his shoes and went out, the untied laces flopping against the deck as he shuffled through the passageway to the port side where he bent over to drink from the scuttlebutt. Wiping his mouth, he ambled past the open door to the old gunners' mess. Cooper was reading a book. Britt was wearing a black rubber slicker and holding a flashlight in his hand. Chips was playing pinochle. The Bosun looked at his watch. It was nearly sunset. Britt was about to go forward on lookout. The Ordinary Seaman had to be on the wheel. Going back to his room, the Bosun hesitated outside the door to the four-to-eight focsle. Cautiously he rapped lightly before opening it a crack.

Cynthia was lying on her side, facing the bulkhead, covered up to her neck with a sheet tucked around her body. The Bosun closed the door, licking his lips, his breath whistling slightly as he exhaled with sudden gasps, both hands rubbing his erection as his knees pranced nervously. Slowly he pulled down the sheet, bending his head to peer underneath at Cynthia's naked buttocks. The Bosun jerked. There was a chain around her waist. Fastened to the chain with a padlock was a bent iron bar two inches wide jammed between the cheeks of her buttocks.

He grabbed the doll by her hip and rolled her over, staring at the semicircle of iron that went between her legs, the other end connected to the chain by a second padlock. Angrily, he tried to pull her down off the bunk. But both wrists were fastened to the frame of the bunk with a set of handcuffs. Desperately the Bosun pulled and jerked at her legs until they dangled over the deck, her back bent over the edge of the mattress. Her arms were stretched over her head, her open eyes staring at him without expression. He looked at her, gasping. He punched her in the stomach. And then again, with a quick and vicious jab.

Whore! Bitch! Not good enough for you, huh?

He tried to grab her around the neck, pressing against her throat with his stumps and his knuckles. Then he hit her in the face, once, twice. Cynthia's body flopped loosely, her hair disarrayed, the handcuffs rattling as the frame of the bunk shook and banged in its supports. The Bosun breathed heavily, a thin trail of saliva dripping out of the corner of his lips as he hissed and sputtered.

Won't let me in. Huh? Yeah? *Yeah?*

Deliberately holding his breath to regain his self-control, he opened and closed the door quietly. He went back to his room. He picked up a bucket of tools and set it down on the bench, pawing among the grease gun and the Zerk and Alemite fitting attachments, a crescent wrench, a topping maul and then the sail-canvas sheath that held a marlin spike and a knife. He returned to the four-to-eight focsle. He snatched out the marlin spike and held it in his left hand, braced against his finger stumps by his thumb. Staring at the sharp, flattened tip, he flexed his jaws and hissed.

How's this for a prick? Huh? Really king-size. Right?

The Bosun inserted the tip of the spike under the iron bar, working it further in, prying up and down as Cynthia's body flopped back and forth. He could feel the tip tearing through her flesh and tissue, hammering repeatedly on the round, flat handle with his fist until half its length was inside. And then he stepped back with a malevolent grin.

Stiff enough for you, Cynthia? Huh?

With a short, swallowed whimper, he snatched out the sheath knife. Holding it up in both hands, he plunged it deep into the doll's chest. Working it out, he stabbed her again. And again. Suddenly he began slashing and stabbing blindly, relentlessly, whimpering and whining and gasping for breath.

The knife swung lower. There was dull, sloshing sound as it hit her stomach. And then a quick gush of warm water wet the front of the Bosun's pants and ran down his legs. He stopped, looking down in amazement. He tried to pull the sopping cloth away from his genitals with his one little finger, squirming his hips.

You—pissed—right *on* me. You *pissed* on me!

Left and right, he slashed at Cynthia's stomach and her breasts, digging at her face and her eyes. Making incomprehensible sounds, sobbing, he stood up on the edge of the mattress on the lower bunk, leaned over and began to saw and hack at her shackled wrists, his lips spluttering as he grunted and hissed and whimpered.

● THE SCREAMS BEGAN as a series of agonized howls that built upon each other, becoming louder and louder until they could be heard all over the ship. The Utility-man ran out of the galley, tripping over the bucket of soogee water he had just prepared to scrub down the deck. The four pinochle players came running out of the mess-hall. The twelve-to-four watch tumbled out of the focsle, the Deacon dropping his Bible to leap down from his top bunk, clutching at the crotch of his jockey shorts; Whitey cursing and Reggie rubbing the sleep out of his eyes. There was an immediate crowd in the passageways, wip-ers, firemen and oilers, cooks and messmen, all of them terrified by those unnatural sounds of anguish but none daring to come closer to Vytas as he stood there holding the amputated left hand of the doll tenderly cupped in his own, its wrist crudely hacked off, the palm and curled fingers turned up.

Tu vuzaņķi! Tu beidzot tomēr to izdariji! Tu nevari saskatit neko labu nevienā vietā. Nenostiecīgs-nenovēligs. Tu nevari pielaut ka kāds nabaga ieceļōtājs var izvīrzities tev priekšā. Jūs neko vēlīgie amerikaņi.

Up on the officers' deck engineers and mates were putting on shoes, wrapping themselves with towels, pull-ing on unzipped khaki pants to come tumbling down the ladder. The Third Mate saw Vytas haranguing the hud-dled crew, his furious screams more and more fluent, his phrases emphasized and lilting.

Viņš nokāvēja viņu! Viņš nokāvēja Mara! Manu dār-gumu. Viņa tak bija mana. Es viņu atradu un viņs mežonīgi sagrieza viņu ar nazi. Tur nu viņa guļ miruse. Mana mīlule. Vazaņkis! Viņs nonāvēja manu sievu.

Vytas yelled directly at first one man and then another. Some hung their heads and some flinched away. Others could not keep from grinning. Still others stiffened and stared into the twisted distortions of each other's faces. Vytas spun around and ran back to the focsle. The crew cautiously followed. But there was a sudden stampede, everyone stumbling and stepping on the feet of those behind him, when Vytas reappeared, wildly swinging a sheath knife.

Tu paklīdušais. Tu sevi par daudz augstu vērtē. Tavs krekls jau tomēr smird pa gabalu.

Again he lunged, cutting viciously, the front ranks of the crowd stumbling and trying to shoulder their way through the mass of bodies. And again there was a sobbing scream from Vytas, chilling, shrill—

Nazi! Nazi! *Nazi!* Ha? You Nazi guy, you. Ha? Jā. Kāpēc tu nekā nesaki. Vai tu esi tik dumjš? Neproti runāt? Neizglītots. Muļķies.

Vytas made a sudden charge down the starboard passageway. Reggie leaped aside, ducking into the black gang shower. Sanitary Sam fumbled desperately with the doorknob of the Wipers' focsle before getting it open and stumbling inside.

Bastit! No gut some bitch.

Vytas stopped and slowly retreated to his own focsle, looking warily over his shoulder. A few men followed him but kept their distance, flinching with suspicion whenever he hesitated. He went inside. In a moment he came out, carrying the doll in his arms. He stood there in the middle of the passageway, sobbing, the knife in his hand but no longer a threat, the crew standing still, staring at the slashed breasts and legs, the amputated wrist, the gaping stomach with the punctured bladder hanging out of the wound, the padlocks and chain, the iron bar, the loose flap of skin and pubic hair that revealed the ruined genitalia, the face mutilated with numerous cuts and holes. Granulated crumbs of foam rubber fell out of the stab wounds and onto the deck as Vytas shivered with his weeping convulsions. The doll's head twisted and her left eye clattered to the deck, hitting against a bulkhead and spinning away. The ship rolled to starboard. The eye turned, staring at the silent, horrified seamen. The ship creaked, hesitated and recovered, beginning its roll to port, the shining blue eye moving away, clinking sharply against the stanchion that supported the ladder rail, twisting, staring again and then rolling against Whitey's shoe.

Mara! Mara! MARA!

Weeping and moaning piteously, Vytas staggered forward, the crew shifting, making no attempt to interfere with his clumsy progress toward the storm door at the after end of the house. Several men followed him outside on the main deck. They watched him stumble out into the darkness and the beams of light emanating from various portholes. He stepped up on a mooring bitt and then placed one foot on top of the bulwarks, his contorted face looking down at the doll and then out over the sea, the wind mussing his hair. And then in one quick motion he jumped over the side.

MAN OVERBOARD!

The cry was picked up and repeated and sent back over the deck, through the passageways and up the ladders to the wheelhouse, where the Chief Mate himself began to answer the yells, startled and shaken.

Man overboard! Man overboard! Starboard side. Come hard *right!* Hard right *rudder!*

With desperation Cooper began pawing at the spokes of the wheel. Mister Delray ran out on the starboard wing. He made a false start back to the wheelhouse, then returned to look over the side again, his fingers shaking as he tried to remember all those things he had written down as answers to the hundreds of questions on his various examinations as Third Mate, as Second Mate, as Chief Mate and finally once again for his Master's license; things he should be doing now, instantly and simultaneously. Yet all he could think of were the words "Williamson Turn. Williamson. Williamson." He turned to the wheelhouse, leaping through the open door and pushing over the red handle of the general alarm to lock it in place. Bells began ringing all over the ship. He ran out the door again to the wing, where he jerked at a life ring to throw it over the side. But the ring merely fell a few feet, swinging by the line fastened to the water light. He grabbed the can with both hands and jerked it. The ring pulled out and both the ring buoy and the flare were free in his hands. He hesitated, turned his head and yelled:

How are you heading now, Cooper?

Three-zero-*zero*—zero-*three*—zero-*six*—

The Mate repeated the headings to himself, calculating, trying to be calm and to think. Three-zero-six. That's sixty degrees off course. *Sixty?* Oh, Christ!

Hard *left!* Come hard left! Hard over! *Quick!*

Cooper slapped at the spokes of the wheel, which began to spin, assisted by the back pressure of the telemotor pistons. The pointer of the rudder indicator quickly came back to midships as Cooper began straining again to turn the wheel all the way to the left. The Chief Mate could feel the ship beginning to heel under the force of the sudden turn. He stepped inside the wheelhouse, the ring buoy still in his hands. The hundred-foot coil of manila line had come undone, trailing behind his feet in a mass of kinks and tangled bights. The Second Mate came running in, carrying his shirt, his shoe laces untied, his chest heaving as he fought for breath.

Did you get the *time?* Did you get it? Have you got the bell book? Where's the god-damn bell book?

The Second Mate ran out the door, colliding with the

Captain, who was barefooted and bare-chested, wearing only a pair of khaki pants with the fly open.

What the fuck's goin' *on*? What's *hap*pening?

Man overboard, Captain. Man *over*board.

Turn off that god-damn general alarm. So I can think.

Captain Pedersen went out on the wing. Ignoring the presence of the Chief Mate, he put one naked foot on the running-light box and looked over the side. Off on the port quarter, just to the right of the circling wake, he could see the white glow of a water light from a ring buoy. The Captain went back into the wheelhouse, twisting the gyro repeater around to watch the ship's heading swing to the left, moving through zero-eight-five toward the reciprocal of their original course. The Chief Mate heard the whir and the clatter of the engine-room telegraph as the Captain pulled the handle back and forth, bringing it to STOP, at the same time ordering the wheel amidships. The Chief Mate grunted and heaved the ring buoy over the side. There was a plop on the water and then the sudden glow of the flare as the chemicals in the can mixed with sea water, reacted and ignited.

The Captain's voice boomed out of the darkness:

Did you throw that fuckin' buoy over just then?

Yes, sir. Yes, sir. It was I. It was me.

What the hell's the matter with you? *Now* you throw it over? What good is that? That other water light was thrown over before you even began your turn.

But it's way to the left of our original course.

The wind's southwest, ain't it? It *blew* it off course. A ring buoy is lighter than a loaded ship. We're deeper down in the water. Right? Well, god damn it. Right or not?

Yes. Yes, sir. Okay.

Okay? Shit, yes, it's okay. Wait a minute. I'll take over the con. You go out and put the fuckin' cargo lights on.

But we'll be blinded.

We can't see more'n a hundred feet, anyway. It's *night*time. Didn't you notice? No? But it *will* give the man in the water a chance to see *us*.

The telephone rang. The Mate pulled out the receiver.

Bridge? Yeah. We got a man overboard. How the hell do I know? Yeah. We'll be maneuvering. What do you think?

The Chief Mate went to the switch panel and turned on the lights on the boat deck. Running below to the officers' deck, he switched on the lights to the outside passageways. He went down to the main deck and saw Whitey, yelling at him as he turned and ran back topside.

Quick. Go out and switch on all the cargo lights.

Captain Pedersen cupped his hands together, stuck his head through the open porthole and took a deep breath, his voice booming out over the foredeck to the bow:

BRITT? GO UP THE FOREMAST LADDER. GO *ALOFT*. UP TO THE CROSSTREES. WE NEED A LOOKOUT UP *HIGH*.

A flashlight went on and off. The Captain turned.

Cooper? You still got steering way?

Yes, sir. A little.

How's your heading?

Sixty. And still coming left.

What were you steering before? Two-four-six?

Yes, sir.

Very well. Check her. And try to hold her as steady as you can on sixty-six.

Yes, sir. Steer zero-six-six.

The Second Mate stood in the corner, scribbling in the bell book, the end of a flashlight held in his mouth.

Symons? Put that crap away and run down and call out all hands. Start preparin' number one boat for launching. And get 'em all to put on their life jackets. Now scram. *Fast.*

Yes, *sir.*

The Third Mate was trying to button his shirt.

Teier? Go get my personal binoculars. In my room. They're hangin' on a hook over my bed. But shit. Let's face it. There ain't a Chinaman's chance of findin' a man out there now. How did it happen? Weather's good. He wasn't workin' on deck at this hour. He couldn't be drunk. Was he crazy? Did he flip? Who the hell was it, anyway?

Mister Teier answered from the door.

Johan Vytas. The four-to-eight Ordinary.

So? What happened?

Nobody's exactly sure. It looks like somebody threw his doll over the side. And he went in after it.

For a long moment the Captain didn't answer. When he did speak, his voice quavered and went hoarse:

That *doll?* That god-damn fuckin' *doll?* So? She finally did it. Oh, Christ. I should have known. I knew all the time I should have given her the deep six.

The Captain cleared his throat and snuffled his nose. His voice dropped lower, became resonant and tough:

Jesus Christ. What next? Huh?

The Third Mate returned with the binoculars, gave them to the Captain, took the ship's glasses out of the box and began scanning the horizon. The Captain growled, his voice strangled and muted:

Teier? Ring slow ahead.

Slow ahead, sir.

The Third Mate leaped for the telegraph and pushed the handle forward. The bell rang as the engine room answered, the pointer stopping at SLOW. There was a slight shudder in the deck as the pistons began to move up and down.

Damn it to hell. It's really *my* fault. I'm responsible for all those morons. *Me.* The Master is *always* to blame.

Captain Pedersen raised his binoculars.

Steady as she goes, Cooper.

Steady, sir.

That life ring is over there, Cap'n. To the left.

I know. But it's on the surface. A man is deep in the water. He'll drift the same way a ship would. I want to look over here first.

But he would swim *toward* the light, Cap'n.

Yes. True. Good point. *If* he could see it. And if *he* was sane. But if he *jumped* over. Then he'd be too nutty to predict what he'd do. Shit. It's like lookin' for a needle in a haystack. Findin' a man in the open sea after dark. Stop the ship.

Stop her, sir.

Come left easy.

Come left easy, Cap'n.

Cooper? That was your watch partner, wasn't it?

Vytas? Yes, sir.

Was he a nut?

Cooper stammered slightly, coughed once and then spoke:

I don't know, Captain. You couldn't tell. He was a little weird, maybe. But nothin' unusual.

Cooper stretched, craning his neck as he tried to look through the portholes at the sea, muttering very quietly:

That poor little prick.

The Captain heard the catch in Cooper's voice. He came closer, peering into his face, the light from the binnacle dimly showing the tears rolling down his cheeks. Cooper snuffled his nose and wiped it with his sleeve. Captain Pedersen reached out, gripping him by the shoulder with a tight squeeze. As soon as he touched him, Cooper started bawling with a short, loud wail. The Captain's hand relaxed. Gently he patted Cooper's arm.

Yes, boy. I know. Take it easy.

A voice began calling from the main deck. The Captain put his head through the porthole and saw Whitey below.

I can't put the lights on. The masthouses are locked.

Who's got the key?

The Bosun's got 'em.

So where the hell's the Bosun?

I can't find him.

You can't find him? Well. *Look* for him. No. Wait. There's a ring of master keys on the Chief Mate's desk. Use those.

The darkness on the boat deck was filled with jostling shapes, the pounding of feet, heavy breathing, a jumble of orders, questions and curses. Whiskey Bill saw the Second Engineer run out of his room and disappear through the door to the fidley. Cautiously he crept inside the deck house. One of the officers had left his door on the hook, the lights on in his room. Whiskey Bill went inside, lifted up the foot of the mattress and ran his hand underneath, groping for one of the bottles.

The Second Mate yelled up to the bridge, number one lifeboat already over the side, swinging from the falls.

Ready to lower away, Captain.

Very well. Stand by. We have to find him first.

Cooper yelled from inside the wheelhouse:

I got no more steerageway, Cap'n. She won't answer.

Dead slow ahead, Mister Teier.

Dead slow ahead, sir.

The Chief Mate got the cover off the searchlight on top of the flying bridge, switched it on and began sweeping back and forth over the water.

Cooper kept shifting his gaze away from the small lighted segment of the gyro compass. Rubbing his eyes with his knuckles and snuffling his nose, he looked through the wheelhouse portholes at the searchlight beam nervously playing over the black expanse of sea. He tried not to think of Vytas actually being out there. He tried to think of something else, to think of getting relieved at the end of his watch, of going below to his bunk and to the earphones of his radio.

He even tried closing his eyes and letting his mind

go blank. But when he did, he could still see the old woman, undimmed by his tears, by memory, by intoxication. She was hunched and crooked, carrying a very large carpetbag overflowing with assorted junk with makeshift handles of frayed greasy rope. Her shoulders were bony and stubborn, stiffly holding up the ragged gray dress. Her feet were in blue sneakers, her gray hair almost hidden inside an ancient cloche hat of purple flannel.

Cooper staggered forward, holding out his arms.

Mother!

The old woman glared at him. Squinting her eyes, she went on, her lips moving rapidly. Cooper followed, his twitching hands hovering close to her arm.

It's *me*. Don't you remember? Up the street?

The hag quickened her step, her shoulders hunched high, her head pulled down, snapping at him through clenched teeth:

Beat it. Cryin' out loud. Whaddaya want? Huh? Go wan. Scram or I'll call a cop. Go wan. Huh?

But, Mother. It's me. Mark. Your *baby*.

Go wan, willya? Go pick on somebody your own age. Jeez. Ain'tcha got no kind o' respect?

Cooper could still remember the bum standing there on the sidewalk, staring. He took one last gurgle of the whiskey, his hands trembling. He shook his head rapidly. He blinked.

When Britt reached the top of the foremast ladder, he pulled himself up on the crosstrees, clinging tightly to the guardrail and gasping for breath. He never liked to go aloft at any time, but now it was night and the ship was rolling heavily. He looked down at the deck below and then out over the blackness and the foam and the crests of the seas, the wind pulling at his clothes, cold against his face and hands. The sky was clear and even small-magnitude stars were visible. There was a strong glow in the east, the moon about to break the horizon.

The cargo lights on the foremast went on with a sudden flash. Whitey moved aft to the mainmast, unlocked the door to the house and went inside with his flashlight. He went back to the after deck house. He flipped the switches in the box in the narrow passageway and then noticed that the padlock on the door to the lazaret was open. He went inside, suspicious, training his flashlight around the dark storeroom. The Bosun was sitting on a rolled-up tarpaulin, holding his mutilated hands in front of his face, whimpering as he gnawed at the stumps of his fingers.

Whitey turned off the flashlight and went to the door, his voice mocking, his leer invisible in the darkness:

Bosun? Ya know somethin'? You're a sentimental slob.

The Captain conned the ship in a large circle, trying to calculate every possible effect of wind and current, of time, speed and drift. Finally he began blowing the whistle, pulling down on the overhead handle, a sputtering of condensed steam turning into a roar. Captain Pedersen waited. He raised a megaphone to his ear, turning slowly from side to side, trying to pick up the slightest, most distant cry.

The whistle blew again, reverberating, long and immense in the night. Trembling, Britt let go of the guardrail on the crosstrees, putting his hands over his ears and opening his mouth wide to relieve the pressure of the sound. Then he grabbed the rail to hang on tight as he swung through the air in a great arc, the ship sluggishly rolling in the trough of the sea.

Easing the rudder and increasing the speed to half ahead, the Captain turned through still larger circles, the whistle blowing with lengthening, despairing intervals. And then there was a cry from the lookout, an incoherent shriek. The Captain's voice boomed out through the wheelhouse porthole:

205

WHAT? *WHAT?*

Over there! There they are! I see 'em!

WHERE ARE THEY?

Over there. Over there.

WHERE THE *HELL* IS THAT?

Three points. Three points off the port bow.

The searchlight moved to Britt's indicated bearing, shifting slightly until it settled on two objects close together in the water. Captain Pedersen and the Third Mate ran out on the port wing of the bridge and raised their binoculars.

Hard left, Cooper.

Hard left, sir.

The ship drew closer and swung around with its engine stopped, the hull forming a lee for the boat on the starboard side. The crew lined the bulwarks, watching Vytas as he swam away from them with a desperate side-stroke, towing the doll by the hair. The boat was being lowered, the falls squeaking, the men yelling at each other in confusion and in anger. Captain Pedersen spoke through the megaphone in a clear, firm and reasonable voice:

VYTAS. WAIT FOR US. WE'RE SENDING A BOAT OVER TO PICK YOU UP. VYTAS. WAIT. JUST RELAX.

There was a faint, indistinct scream coming over the water. But the tone was defiant, in pain, hysterical.

Inside the wheelhouse, Cooper began to yell, his voice excited, hoarse, strangled with tension:

Captain? Captain Pedersen?

The Captain ran inside from the wing.

Yeah? What is it? What is it?

Let me go out in the boat, Captain. He'll listen to me.

Captain Pedersen hesitated.

Please, sir.

Mister *Teier?*

Yes, sir?

Stand by the wheel.

Cooper ran out of the wheelhouse and down the ladder to the boat deck. He leaned over the side and grabbed one of the manropes that hung from the cable between the two davits, quickly climbing down toward the boat, using the big overhand knots for foot and hand holds. As soon as he settled in the bows, the falls were released.

The Chief Mate screamed one order after the other, insulting them all, threatening them, pleading and encouraging and cursing at the crew, who cursed right back at him and at each other, banging oars and boat hooks, scraping their feet on the grating and kicking against the flotation tanks with a cacophony of thuds and clangs and rattles, yelling in shouts of pain when scraped and banged by each other's oars and knees and elbows. With jerking spasms, the boat got underway, rolling and pitching in the seas, the spray flying back into their faces with every stroke. The Second Mate carried a heavy emergency lantern, playing it over the water, following the beam of the ship's searchlight. As the lifeboat rose up on the crest of a wave, Cooper could see Vytas and the doll up ahead.

Vytas! Vytas! Hold on! We're coming!

There was a faint sound of angry invective, an interruption, a pause, one last shout and then silence. Cooper yelled again. There was no answer. The bow of the boat rose up to meet the next sea, but Cooper could only see the doll.

The boat pulled alongside. She floated in a bent, awkward position, weighted at her center of gravity by the heavy iron of the chastity belt, the buoyancy gone from the ruptured bladder, both arms extended, the knees and feet just breaking the surface. The sailors sat by their oars in silence, the disfigured, one-eyed face staring up

207

at them, half submerged, illuminated by the Second Mate's lantern and by the glow of the moon, which had just broken the horizon.

In a low, confidential voice, Cooper tried again, speaking to the nearby sea and the darkness:

Vytas? Are you there?

There was a long pause. Very quietly Whitey spoke to no one in particular, his voice respectful and soft:

Shall we take her back? Maybe—with glue and stuff and the right kind of clamps—you know—rubber cement and—

Cooper's reply was not so much to Whitey as it was to the sea:

Let her go. Maybe somebody else will find her. And adopt her—or—you know—put her back together. Or maybe she'll just float. Just drift . . . with the current . . .

The crew was motionless, their faces round and solemn and without features in the gleam of the rising moon, the Chief Mate slumped over the tiller, the sailors clinging to their oars.